REVEL

A CURVY SEDUCTION SAGA PREQUEL

AIDY AWARD

ACKNOWLEDGMENTS

I have to give an extra shout out to Corinne A. for doing one last proofread for me. The book is better because you care. Hugs.

Thank you so much for my VIP fans for all their love and support for me and every story I write. You're so very important to me.

Extra hugs to you ~

- Daphine G.
- Debbie Joy G.
- Heather R.
- Kerrie M.
- Michele C.

And great big thanks to my official biggest fan ever~
Hugs and Kisses for you!

- Helena E.

REVEL

GRAY'S SEDUCTION

Gray:

I've been Angelina's bodyguard for years and in lust with her since the day we met. When she finally kicks her stupid fiancé to the curb I've got a chance to finally make her mine.

But I won't be her rebound.

I will help her find that kinky desirable side of herself. Even if means sacrificing my own happiness.

*For everyone who never quite got over
that one book boyfriend*

Beauty and seduction, I believe,
is nature's tool for survival,
because we will protect
what we fall in love with.

—Louie Schwartzberg

FUCKED

*T*hree little words. Every woman wanted to hear them. Three words are all it took for any woman to be mine. Three tiny words that I love to say—Come for me.

Since the day I discovered I had the power to make a woman climax, the one thing guaranteed to always turn me the fuck on was a woman's O-face. Whether she was mouth round and open wide screaming my name, scrunched up like an angry-looking Shar-Pei, or my personal favorite - the lip-biter who can't keep her eyes on mine even though she will get her ass spanked for disobeying my order but it's too fucking good - I loved every single one. Because I was sending her mind and body into blissful orbit, and she belonged to me. Her body and soul, in that moment, were mine.

Except tonight and every night for the past month. Beautiful women in various states of arousal surrounded me. The most desirable submissives who wanted nothing more than to let me do every dirty thing in the dirtiest of books to them, and I didn't want to fuck a single one of them.

Couldn't care less if I made them come.

I had the ability get any of them off or have them begging to be allowed to orgasm. Even the toughest brat went so far into subspace she'd forget her name and then I'd pull her back with the gentle touch of aftercare. All without a tingle of interest from my own damn cock.

Fuck my life.

Maybe BDSM wasn't my thing anymore.

"Sir?"

I looked up from the now watery glass of whiskey I'd been nursing for half an hour. A rail thin woman with big, bouncy, had-to-be-fake tits, wearing only the collar designating her as an Asylum house slave, knelt before me. All I thought was how she needed to eat a cheeseburger or something. God, I was such a dick, not fit to be with anyone, much less dominate them.

"Master Bennett sent me as a gift to use as you please. How may I serve you?"

Fucking Bennett. This woman was no gift. She was a taunt.

It had been three years, four months, and twenty-nine days since we'd gotten out of the VA hospital. My body had been healed three years, four months, and twenty-two of those. Foster Bennett's not as long. Not at all.

Bennett wouldn't let me forget that for even a minute.

I'd love nothing more than to tell this sub to take the night off, just to piss on Bennett's parade. This little submissive had signed up to be used, but not like that.

I glanced around the club to see who I might pawn her off on.

There were plenty of other Doms around, and I not a single one looked my way. Not even Jackass Jim, who loved to give a good spanking, had his back to me. No doubt I had Bennet to blame for that too. Shit.

Damn. If Delta Force had taught me one thing, it was how to improvise. It wasn't like I didn't know what to do with her, I just didn't want to. I could give her pleasure, no problem, but there would be none in it for me. "What's your name, darlin'?"

"Sir?"

"No, that's what you'll call me when you're coming."

She blinked like she was surprised by that. How long had she been in the lifestyle? Not long enough to deal with the likes of me.

"When I ask you a question, you answer verbally. No thinking, stay out of your head. Got it?"

She nodded.

I didn't move except to raise one eyebrow.

She swallowed. "Yes, sir."

"Good girl. Now, what's your name?"

"Celine."

Pretty name. Pretty girl. If she didn't smarten up, she would get taken advantage of in all the wrong ways.

"Safe word?" Not that I thought she'd need it. Not tonight, not with me. I wasn't interested in pushing her limits.

"Red."

"Any hard limits out of the ordinary big ones like no blood, no scat, etcetera?"

She swallowed again, and I reconsidered playing her at all.

"No, Sir."

Wrong answer. She was on my lap with her legs spread before she even blinked. I held a chunk of her hair tight and wrapped my other hand around her throat. She instinctively grasped my arm, her eyes dilated, skirting the line between arousal and fear.

Her pulse raced beneath my palm and I pressed against her skin. Not enough to restrict her breathing, just enough to see if this was her kink.

She parted her lips then licked them trying to be sexy, but I recognized fear when I saw it. She wanted me to think she liked this.

Did I care?

Not really.

But she did, or at least needed to pretend she liked this. I might have a black soul, but it was good for putting the fear of God in sweet, innocent, naïve things. Celine needed a little fear.

I tightened my grip on her throat and whispered in her ear. "Everyone has hard limits and I don't like your answer. So, we're going to work on it."

Jesus, was that my voice?

"But... Yes, sir."

Damn, she was so green. I ought to scare her all the way out of this lifestyle. I could. Push those limits she thought she didn't have. Ruin her. Destroy her. I knew how to be that guy.

I hated what Bennet had become. I was worse.

Who the fuck was I to talk anyone out of doing what they want? I thought I could help. I was wrong.

"Good girl." She wanted to experience a Dom. I could give her that. There wasn't much else I had for anyone.

"One hand between your legs. Spread those lips and legs wide for me. Let everyone in here see that pretty pink pussy."

She released my arm and dropped her hand. There was a massive submissive streak in her. She needed someone to take her power away. But she was like so many other greenies. No idea she held all the power.

I didn't need to glance around the club to feel all eyes were on us. Men, and probably a lot of women, lusted after her. Even more would when I was finished with her.

"Don't move another inch, Celine."

The way she froze at my slightest command was beautiful. I wish I wanted her. I wish I felt anything.

I growled out my next words. Celine didn't need to know I had no use for her. "Say it."

"Sorry?"

My voice dropped into darkness. The devil in me itching to get out. "Never apologize."

"Y-yes, sir."

"That's what I want to hear. I won't punish you now, but if you fail to say it again, I will. Do you understand?"

"Yes, sir."

We would see.

"Now. Fingers in your pussy, stroke your clit, nice and slow and tell me if you're wet already or if we need to get you ready."

"Yes, sir."

If I didn't ruin her tonight, she'd be a beautiful sub for someone. Anyone but Bennett. I might be able to destroy her. He would annihilate her. Wipe her out and try to rebuild her in a new twisted image only his sick mind envisioned.

And I was the one who'd made him that way.

"I'm... I'm already wet, sir."

"Let me see." She raised her fingers and they glistened. She was more than wet. She was dripping. For me. I couldn't care less. I needed to find a way to pretend I did, at least for a little while. "Lick those fingers clean. Tell me what you taste like."

She moved her hand to her mouth and touched her lips. I loosened my grip on her hair, prepared to meet out her first taste of my reminder.

We would soon find out if pain was a deterrent or a kink. So far, the only ones I discovered that turned her on was exhibition and my domination.

"Yes, sir."

"Ah. You were this close to feeling the smack of my hand on your pussy."

Celine gasped, the tiniest bit and for such a fleeting moment that if I hadn't been paying attention, I might not have noticed. She wanted the pain.

That was something I could give her.

I'd had every intention of keeping my hands off her, letting her get off on words alone, but in the mood I was in, physical domination would be safer. For her.

"Across my lap, Celine, legs spread wide and those fingers don't leave your pussy unless I saw so."

I released her and she scrambled to comply. Yeah, she wanted this spanking. A lot more than I wanted to give it to her.

She got herself positioned even with the awkward position I demanded of her. Her ass was in the air, her pussy exposed and her fingers were on her clit.

I didn't move a muscle, only waited.

I didn't do pain for punishment. Denial was a much harsher teacher.

Celine squirmed and turned her head to glance back at me. When her eyes met mine, they gaped wide.

"Shit. Sorry. Shit." She sighed, looked away and down at the floor.

Lesson learned.

"Two words, little sub, and I'll give you want you need. Forget them again, and your next punishment will be much more uncomfortable."

"Yes, sir."

Smack. I brought my hand down hard, hitting not just her ass, put that wet pussy too. She groaned exactly like I expected her to.

I gave her two more before her next instruction. "Each time I spank you, stroke your clit. But do not come until I say you can."

"Yes, sir."

She didn't forget this time.

I didn't start in on her slow and gentle. I didn't pepper her ass cheeks with light spankings. I should have. I didn't.

I brought my palm down over her wet pussy over and over, ten, twenty, fifty times, until her skin was red, her legs were shaking, and her groans had become one long wail with her need.

When we began her fingers were eager to flick her clit fast and furious with each spanking, but now her hand and thighs were soaked and she barely touched herself each time.

"Are you ready to come?"

She panted before answering, and her voice came out the tiniest of whimpers. "Yes, sir. Please."

"Not yet."

"Yes, sir."

I spanked her again and again and again. She was on fire. I

was nothing. I had no intention of letting her come, because I was a fucking asshole.

But I was a summer breeze compared to what Bennett would do to her if allowed.

He was watching. Since his plan to fuck with me hadn't worked, he'd want what I had from this sub.

God dammit.

I'd wanted to save her, from Bennet, from herself. Like always, I'd fucked everyone involved.

A mammoth body stepped between Bennett's line of sight and mine. "That's a pretty little sub you've got there, dickhead. You gonna let her come? Or do I have to do it?"

Jackass Jim was like a fucking knight on a white horse. Always coming in to save the day.

Fucker.

I bent over Celine and whispered into her ear one last time. "Come for me. Now."

She exploded, screaming, "Yes, sir."

With her pussy still pulsing from her orgasm, her fingers still pressing on her clit, I picked her up and handed her full-body over to Jim.

"Fuck you, Jackass."

I walked out of The Asylum, knowing Jim would see to Celine's aftercare. He always did the right thing, and I hated him for it.

I used to know what the right thing was. Not anymore.

This was no life. Once upon a time, I'd wanted one. At least I thought I did. Even if I didn't have a clue how to feel anymore, I needed to make a change. Do something good for someone, anyone.

There had to be someone out there who needed me.

ANGEL

*J*esus. This talking head across from me was one slimy piece of shit.

He was going to give me a job on Cruz Enterprises security detail. They wanted former military to be a bodyguard for the owner's daughter. Why these richy-rich types needed protection was beyond me, especially for some little girl.

I was sure she was a spoiled rotten brat, because everyone around here were all a bunch of entitled assholes with pictures of trophy wives on their desks.

Not that I was a whole lot better.

This was like taking money from a baby.

I'd get the brat in line, and it was only five years. I did that kind of time killing terrorists and saving Americans in Delta. I could handle a glorified babysitting position.

Probably.

Cruz and his daughter were just a stepping stone. If I got experience and cash, I could start my own security firm, save lives. Guarding these delicate flowers was hardly what I'd call experience, but the money was unbelievable.

"You'll be on duty twenty-four seven, live at the mansion with her. But I understand a man like you will have," he circled his fingers in the air, "let's say, needs. So, as part of the compensation package, you'll get thirty days off a year and an apartment at Cruz towers for your time off. Twenty percent of the property will be vested for each year of your service."

That apartment alone could fund a dozen security firms. Five years and it was all mine. Then, I'd happily get out, sell the luxury apartment, take the money, and run.

What the hell did I need time off for? I never had much of a life to start off with, even less now if I didn't have the Asylum to go to at night.

"Sounds fine. Where do I sign?"

"Good. My secretary has your NDA, contract, and keys." Slimeball stood and extended his hand to shake mine.

I'd better get over my aversion to pressing the flesh with the sleazy upper crust if I was going to be working for them for the next five years. We shook, and he waved me out to the lobby.

"See Marylin. She'll see to all the details and introduce you to Angie. Take care of that girl and her money, young man. We're all counting on you."

I got the distinct feeling they cared a hell of a lot more about the money than the girl.

Slimeball shut the door before I even got out of his office. I was as glad to rid myself of his disgusting presence.

The woman sitting at the desk, twirling in the chair, was a Marylin all right. Dyed blonde hair contrasted with creamy light brown skin. She was trying to hide her Latin heritage behind that hair, make-up, and designer clothes.

No way those curtains matched the carpet. Regardless, she was fucking gorgeous. Curves in all the right places and a smile that lit up the room.

Jesus. When had I ever cared about a smile? She was sweetness and light, all wrapped up in a body made to be fucked and sucked. By me.

Had Slimeball mentioned anything about fraternization among employees?

That last scene I'd played with Celine popped into my head. Had it been this angel with all the curves in all the right places across my lap, my cock would have been rock fucking hard.

We wouldn't have stopped at one little orgasm either. No. She'd come, again and again, but instead of by her own hand, it would be mine, with my dick deep inside of her.

I'd ride her cunt hard until she screamed my name. Then I'd take her ass. God, that ass.

What was it about this woman that had me feeling something for the first time in... what, months, years?

She caught sight of me on the next spin of the chair and planted her feet, stopping dead. What a pretty pink flamed up her neck and cheeks at getting caught goofing off.

I'd love to see that same blush if I caught her with her hand in her panties after I'd told her not to touch herself. Even better across her ass as I spanked it for her.

"You got something for me, sweet cheeks?" Yeah, I was going there. Nobody had made me sign an office place no sexual harassment policy yet.

"Me?"

"I'll take you, sure." I sat on the edge of the desk and the light scent of her perfume, maybe her shampoo, hit me like a grenade to the brain. Peaches or mangoes.

That blush grew even darker. Mmm.

"No, I—" she stood and tugged on the flowy shirt she wore, which gave me even more of a view of her cleavage. My dick would get lost in between those plump tits.

I should have shut down all those dirty, dirty thoughts I was having about her. In my mind I already had her bent over the desk, fucking her, making her moan.

My cock was so damn happy to have blood flowing to it again, it was completely taking over my brain.

"I meant, I'm not Marylin. She probably went out for a coffee. I was just... uh, biding my time. I've been summoned."

The way she rolled her eyes made me want to laugh at loud at whatever fool had thought to summon her. She might be shy and flustered at the moment, but there was fire in there. God, she would be a fucking challenge and a blast to dominate.

"In trouble with the boss?"

"Ha. Not since I turned eighteen and got the money my mother left me. He just wishes."

If she had money, what was she doing working at a place like this? Working her way up the corporate ladder? No. She barely looked twenty and didn't have that same corporate facade the other women wearing the company boxy man-suit as a uniform embodied.

A woman who had that harried look of an overworked and underpaid secretary rushed into the outer office suite. "Hey, Ange. I see you met your new bodyguard already."

Ange.

Angie.

Angelina Cruz. Daughter of Guillermo Cruz, of Cruz Enterprises. My new boss.

Fuck me.

ENGAGED AND UNENGAGED

$\mathcal{I}$ tried. I fucking tried. The more I stayed cool and reserved around Angelina, the more she wore me down.

I'd been working and living in her expansive mansion for three years and had jacked off more than any normal man should. I'd become a masturbating monk. It wasn't just her incredible curves that had me turned on.

It took a good week of her grumping around, doing her damnedest to lose me, which wasn't possible, and me overhearing a half dozen phone calls to her father about how she didn't need 'no stinking bodyguard' before I caught her sticking her tongue out at me.

I'd come at least a hundred and ten times since then just thinking about how wide her eyes had gone when I told her there were a lot of things I'd rather have her do with that tongue, but none of them would stop me from protecting her.

That god-damned tongue of hers. Her mouth was damn near perfect with those pouty lips that were begging to be fucked.

Something else had happened in the past couple of years. Yeah, I still wanted to fuck her so bad I practically tasted her sweet pussy on my lips. I'd also gotten to appreciate her. The real Angel.

There was only so much distance I could put between us when we were together 24/7. She was the one who'd finally broken the ice when she'd bought us hot fudge sundaes after one of her swanky social events at her country club and made me sit on the back of the car looking at the city lights with her.

I hated that she felt like she had to eat rabbit food and wear those God-awful control top panty-hose to fit in with the bitches and assholes her father spent time with.

She tried to be fake and bubble-headed around them. She wasn't though, and they resented her for it.

Her chestnut brown hair, her exotic-to-them Latin skin, and her curves insulted them. Everything that wasn't their gluten-free white-bread world got under their skin like a bug that needed to be exterminated.

If she didn't own fifty-one percent of Cruz Enterprises and finance all their little golf outings and charity fundraisers, they wouldn't think twice about her.

Which would have been fine by me. The way they looked at her behind her back… with more than disdain, it was pure malice. That alone would have persuaded me to keep this job.

She needed protecting. Not from unknown assailants or thieves, but from the real nasties, the ones who wanted to steal something much more precious.

Nobody put baby in a corner.

They sure as hell were trying to fuck around with my girl. Like tonight. The party of the century.

The announcement of her fucking engagement.

I'd never once in my entire career called in sick. I almost did tonight. Stay home and give myself the brown bottle flu and nurse my fatal case of blue balls.

Instead, I was here waiting for Angel to finish getting ready for this joke of a celebration.

"Gray, please clasp this? I can't get my fingers to stay still. I'm so nervous."

Angelina held out an arm to me with a diamond bracelet that surely cost more than my monthly salary.

"No need to be nervous. I'll be right beside you the whole night." Except the inevitable part later in her bedroom.

"I know. Thank you. It's just that Mindy said I should have worn the black dress because it's slimming, but Marc's favorite color is blue."

Mindy needed to eat a bag of dicks as far as I was concerned. She was a shitty ass best friend to Angel, and I'd spent a lot of time recently monitoring Mindy's extra-curricular activities. She hadn't done anything to hurt Angel so far. She would.

I buckled the bracelet and held her wrist a little too long. "You look stunning in the blue."

"What if he hates my hair?" She touched her carefully done-up hair do as if it would break.

I hated it. Mindy had talked her into dying it blonde. Said she'd look 'so Marilyn'. What Mindy meant was that Angelina would be more like all the other women at the country club, but with curves.

I could lose myself in her curves.

Not that she ever showed them off. Especially since she'd started dating Sparky McFuckface.

This guy was a serious douchebag. Thought he was God's gift to the country club with his fancy ass degree from Yale.

A little negging and she'd become putty in his slimy hands. Yeah, she did have gorgeous brown eyes. Sparky never even came up with anything better than calling her his brown-eyed girl.

What the fuck did she see in him?

She could do so much better.

Except Angel didn't think so, and therein lay the problem. She had no idea how beautiful and desirable she was because no one in her life ever told her that.

Until Marc, who filled her head with backhanded compliments.

I'd been this close to slugging him after the first words that ever came out of his mouth around her.

"Nice ass, jiggle it on over here."

All I did was make sure they didn't physically hurt her or put her in any danger.

Because while Marc was a conniving asshole who would cheat on her every chance he got, Angel needed to learn that lesson all on her own.

Nothing I said would make her see any different.

Because I wasn't her nanny. I was her bodyguard and nothing more.

Because I was the asshole who couldn't have her.

The party went off without a hitch. For Angelina, anyway. Once we arrived at the club and Marc paraded her around on his arm for everyone to congratulate, Angel calmed down.

All she needed in her life was a little acceptance. A little love.

Marc wasn't the right guy to give it to her.

But neither was I.

I could fuck her, open up that seductive siren she hid beneath clothes that were baggy and self-deprecating humor. Seeing her here tonight with all these smarmy bastards who called her the names behind her back almost had me pulling her away from all this.

I could take her to the club. Technically, I was still a member of the Asylum. She'd be shocked as hell.

Bennett had turned his little fuck club into a coveted place that the rich and famous couldn't buy their way into. Only kicky fuckers were allowed through his doors, and only by recommendation from a current member.

I'd had my fair share of Doms, Dommes, subs, and switches knocking on my door for a word from me. Half of them didn't appreciate what the fuck they were asking for. The ones who did, I sent to Jackass. He'd get them in if they were right for the Asylum.

Angelina on her knees, just for me, with nipple and clit clamps, her hands tied behind her back and a yes, sir on her lips would have to be one more fantasy. One which I'd be using to jack off.

Later tonight when she was tucked safely into bed.

Right now, I needed to keep my head in the game. Angel was chatting up some friend of her father's who was leering a little too much down the front of her dress.

Not on my watch.

I approached them and cleared my throat. "Angelina, can I please see you for a moment?"

The leerer didn't like my interruption. Tough.

I held her elbow and guided her away before she even answered.

"Oh my God. Thank you. If I had to hear one more time why Cruz Enterprises needs to invest in that old windbag's media company, I was going to fake fainting. You had perfect timing." She rolled her eyes and took a deep cleansing breath. "Have you seen Marc?"

Douchebag should have been the one to save her from boring conversations at their own engagement party. "No, but I can make a sweep for him."

"Would you? I feel like I haven't even seen him all night except at the beginning of the reception."

I gave her a salute. "Will do. How much longer do you want to stay?"

"Umm, I don't know. Let me check with Marc first."

Whenever she was around him, that was always her answer. I hated it.

I had to get him out of her life.

To protect her. Not because I was a selfish bastard who wanted her to myself.

Mindy had been scooting her way toward the edge of the room for at least a half an hour. She thought nobody was paying attention. She was wrong. After a quick glance at Angelina, she made a break for the hallway that led to the posh restrooms.

I did not like the look of that.

"Snag me a piece of cake, will ya? I'll make that sweep and meet you by the tower of champagne."

She nodded and rolled her eyes. "Can you believe that crap? What a waste of good bubbles."

Angel headed toward the bar, and I moved in the opposite direction. No sign of Mindy in the hall, but it didn't take me long to find them.

They hadn't even bothered to lock the door.

My years of special forces training and ops were not needed to sneak up on Marc and Mindy. They were oblivious to the world around them.

Mostly because Marc had his cock buried in Mindy's ass.

"Fuck, Mindy. That's right, take my cock, you little whore. Take it all."

"Oh, God. Yes. Call me your whore again."

Bingo.

No surprise these two were into degradation. I'm sure Marc thought he was a big bad Dom. A lot of men could have given Mindy what she needed better than this schmoe.

I hid myself behind the door and pulled out my phone. This was precisely the fodder I needed to get Marc out of Angelina's life for good.

Blackmail was a bitch.

Angel would be hurt when he broke off the engagement. That couldn't be helped. I'd ensure sure he made it perfectly clear he was the problem in their relationship.

Thirty seconds of watching these two screw was more than I ever needed and plenty to keep as my compelling evidence of why Marc was going to suddenly develop a need to go find himself, in a place far away, like Antarctica.

I silently backed out of the restroom and returned to the party. Now, to find Angel and get her the hell out of here.

She wasn't by the champagne, or the cake, or anywhere else in the ballroom.

"Hey, did you guys see which way Angelina went?"

The group of suits I approached snickered and scoffed. One of them motioned toward the ladies' restrooms.

Shit.

The bathrooms shared vents. What was being said in one filtered through to the other.

I sprinted across the room and caught Angel coming out. She was pale and kept swallowing like she was seconds from throwing up.

"Gray." Her voice rasped like a whisper raked over shards of a broken mirror.

"Angel." I wasn't supposed to know anything. She was feeling humiliated and fuck if I would let anyone see that.

"Take me home."

I nodded and moved to put my hand on her arm to lead her away, but she slumped against me, tears forming on her lashes.

"No way, baby. Don't let them see you cry. They aren't worth your tears. Hold your head high and march the fuck out of here."

She glanced up at me and that hurt turned to the fire I'd known she had in her for years. A curt nod and she stood tall, pushing herself off the wall.

I placed my hand on her back and guided her through the people still partying, through the murmurs and whispers, until we were outside, and I could get her into the car.

I directed the driver to take us back to the mansion and then crawled in the back seat with her. Christ, I didn't know what to do.

I wanted to hold her, tell her everything would be all right. She'd be better off without Sparky.

Her body language said not to touch. She was pissed.

Good.

About damn time.

I clenched my fists, containing my own anger. It would feel so damn good to punch in Marc's face. Or worse.

I wouldn't hurt him. Unless she asked me to. Then I'd make him wish he'd never even looked at her.

Angel said nothing the entire ride home. She slammed doors and pretty much shredded her dress, yanking it off as she walked inside. Lord, help Marc if he showed back up here tonight.

Which, of course, the fucktard did.

"Angie? Where the fuck are you? Ange?"

I met Sparky in the front foyer, arms crossed and my face as blank as possible. I kept my tone flat. My fury at him didn't matter. Only Angelina's.

"She's in the great room."

"Thanks. You may not want to stick around for this, man." He said it like we were buddies.

My only tell of my disdain of him was a scant raised eyebrow. "I'm not going anywhere."

Marc shrugged and walked toward where Angelina sat waiting for him. I hope she sprang on his ass like a mother-fucking puma.

She was in adorable pink fluffy pajamas, sipping a mug of tea.

"What the hell, Angie? You left in the middle of the party. We hadn't even made the toasts yet."

"Get out." She didn't raise her voice. No screaming or hysterics for my girl. She was stone cold.

Marc stopped, surprised. Then did his best to play her command off like a joke. "What are you talking about, sweetums?"

Really? He was going to play dumb?

"Get. Out. It's two very simple words, Marc. But I'll spell them out for you if you need me to." Angel didn't even glance at him. She stared at the opposite wall like it was made of trash and dog droppings. "It means leave my house and don't ever come back. Don't call, don't write, do not pass go."

When she finished her explanation, she raised her mug of tea and took a long sip.

Marc dropped into the chair across from her. "I'm not going anywhere. We're getting married, and that's final. Your father already offered me the vice-president of acquisitions position tonight."

I wasn't even a little bit surprised about that. Angelina might own a majority share of the company, but it was as if she didn't exist when it came to running the multi-billion-dollar corporation. She deferred all company business to her misogynistic asshole of a father. Too bad. She would do a better job if given the chance.

I took a post behind Angel and crossed my arms. Sparky needed to see that I had her back. He was already losing his cool.

"Have fun with that. I hear there are lots of boys' trips for the executive team. I'm sure Mindy won't mind if you fuck around with strippers and whores."

"Fuck," Marc whispered under his breath, but we all heard him.

"Look, Angie. It's not like it meant anything. I've got needs, and you aren't filling them. It doesn't mean I don't want to marry you."

Come on, baby. Don't take that shit from him.

Angel didn't say anything, just took another sip of her tea.

"Let's just forget about this entire thing, honey. We can apologize to all the guests tomorrow and tell them you were sick or something."

Fuck that.

Angel took a last swallow from her mug, finishing it off, and set the cup on a side table with a crack.

"Call me honey one more time." Sweetness and light were not the tones dripping from her words.

"Now, Angie, honey. Don't be like that. It's not very attractive."

Angel picked up a small vase, that I happened to know was a fifteenth-century Ming, and threw it at his head.

That's my girl.

Too bad he ducked. "What the hell? Have you gone insane?"

"Grayson." She turned to me and gave me the sweetest smile. "Will you please show Marc out?"

Fuck to the yes I will. "With pleasure."

Marc stood up, falling over himself to get out of my way. "Keep your boy toy away from me."

"We can do this the hard way or the really fucking painful way, asshole. Your choice." I grabbed Marc by the arm and hauled him toward the front door.

"You throw me out and you'll never find anyone else, Angie."

So, he was choosing the painful way. "Shut the fuck up."

Angel grabbed her mug and got up from her chair, following us to the door. "I think I'll be just fine without you."

Yeah, she would.

"Nobody would fuck a fatty like you if it weren't for your

money, Angie. Kick me out and you'll have to start paying for sex." Desperation and my tight grip on his shoulder tinged his voice.

Smug rat-bastard. Time to start feeling that pain. I literally picked Marc up by the collar and threw him out the front door.

Oh yeah, that felt extremely fucking good. I'd do it again and again if I could.

He skidded into the gravel drive and I was damn disappointed he hadn't landed on his pretty boy face.

"You're a fat-whore-rich-bitch and," Marc brushed the bits of gravel off his precious suit and stabbed at Angel some more. "You might as well have your manservant here to take you for a ride. You'll never get anyone else to even flirt with you, with your fucking jelly rolls. Though I doubt his salary is enough to try and squeeze his way between your thunder thighs."

I was going to kill him. I had how to hide a body skills. It would be fine. "I'll give you a three-second head start, Sparky. Just for fun. You'd better start running, rich boy."

I would have laughed at Marc's scared shitless expression, except I didn't get a chance. Angel threw that mug at his face. Unfortunately, it bounced off his thick skull and shattered on the ground next to him.

"Goodbye, Marc."

She grabbed my arm and dragged me back into the house. I got in one last threat, shooting a finger gun at his head, before she slammed the door.

"Thanks." She pressed one hand to the wood and looked up at me.

There was still a lot of hurt and anger in those gorgeous brown eyes. I wanted to kiss them away. I'd wait while she healed.

Then I'd show her how a woman should be treated.

Fuck. Was I actually thinking that?

Yeah. I was.

She was everything I'd wanted for three long damn years.

No promises. No forevers. But I would protect her and help her see she was worth it.

"That's what I'm here for."

The tears shimmered on her lashes. "Good. Now, let's get drunk."

Whoa. Okay, then. That I could do. "You're the boss."

Instead of heading into the kitchen, Angel sauntered back into the great room and pulled a bottle out of the cushions of the chair where she'd been waiting for Marc.

Uh-oh. "You started without me?"

She popped the lid off the tequila and took a swig, not even making a face. Then she held it out to me.

I took the bottle, with zero intentions of giving it back. "Your tea wasn't herbal, was it?"

"Nope. Unless you count agave and worms."

Shit. Was this how she'd stayed so calm when Marc was being a huge dickhead? I should have noticed instead of focusing on revenge fantasies.

"How much have you had?"

She stuck out her jaw. "Enough."

"I agree. Let's get you to bed."

Angel walked right up to me, walked her fingers up the front of my shirt, and tipped her head up, letting me see the best kind of sparkle in her eyes. "Yours or mine?"

Ah, hell.

How the fuck could I resist?

IT'S ABOUT THE SEX

*S*aying no to her was one of the hardest fucking things I did.

Had it been any other day, and had she been sober, I would have had her on my lap moaning my name with my hand between her legs in an instant.

Instead, I was the asshole who decided to tell her I wouldn't be her rebound.

Yeah. Those fucking words came out of my mouth.

Jesus.

I spent the next two days on the receiving end of the silent treatment. Day one wasn't so bad, because Angel had been nursing both a broken heart and a hangover.

Day two came with more smashing of glassware. Mostly gifts from the engagement party.

I was glad to see her get her mad on, work some of it out of her system. It was the evening of the second day that just about killed me.

That's when the tears came.

Great big sobbing ones that she tried her best to hide from

me. God, how I wanted to comfort her. I'd even take her to bed if it would make her stop crying. Even for a little while.

It wasn't the smart choice, for either of us. But I'd do it.

If she hadn't locked me out of her room.

This morning, she'd come to breakfast puffy-eyed, but with a new determination I hadn't seen in her since she'd started seeing Marc.

"We're going out tonight."

"We are?" I didn't like the sound of this.

"Yes. We are going to celebrate my freedom, and you're going to help me."

"Hmm. What did you have in mind?" If it would make her feel better, we'd hit every exclusive club in town.

"You'll see. First, I need to hit the spa to get rid of my puffy eyes and do a little shopping."

Twelve hours later and we were sitting in the limo outside of a dive bar. We would sit there until she got some sense into her head.

She rattled the door handle and tried to unlock it.

"Damn it, Grayson. Let me out of the car."

I turned my head to glare at her. "Angel, listen to the words coming out of my mouth. This is a stupid idea. There are better ways to get revenge. I could just kill Marc, for example."

"That's a sweet offer," she said, trying to keep the enthusiasm for the idea out of her voice.

Did she realize I could do it? That I would. For her.

"I know what I'm doing, and you agreed to help me. No backing out now."

I raised one eyebrow by about two degrees. I had a great fucking poker face, and she knew it. "I agreed to help you have some fun celebrating your freedom from that dickhead."

"Right, and I can't think of a better way than to do all the things Marc never wanted to and, better yet, with a random rebound guy."

Christ, she was going to kill me. She threw that rebound thing right in my face. How the fuck was I supposed to watch her getting it on with another guy?

Yeah, rebound sex, or revenge sex was an excellent cure for a broken heart, but I needed to find another way she could fix hers without the random hook-up.

She flicked the switch to unlock the door. I instantly flipped it back down. This lecture wasn't over yet.

"Your father will want to kill me."

She glared at me for that comment. Her father and his need to hire a bodyguard was always a sore point, and it had been a cheap shot to try and get her mind off of her plan.

Then, I was the stupid one and brought it back up. I needed to know. "If this is about the sex, a one-night stand isn't—"

She held up a hand to silence me. "It's not about the sex."

Oh, really?

"Fine. It's a little bit about the sex."

Hell. I couldn't. I shouldn't. If she wanted this to help her move on, I should be the one to show her what great sex was. At least I'd be in control.

"Let me take you somewhere else more suited to your needs." I hadn't meant for my voice to drop. I didn't want her to think I was being overprotective. I was, but it was better if she thought she had the power in this relationship at the moment.

Her eyes flicked back and forth between mine and I watched and waited while her brain made the connection.

She had no idea of my darker tastes, my kinks, but she wasn't stupid either. A little naïve maybe, but one night under my control and we'd take care of that.

She waved me off. "Let's just go in."

I stared at her, waiting for her to change her mind. She knew exactly what I was suggesting. The question was whether she wanted it.

Wishful thinking had me being stupid. She wasn't ready.

It wouldn't take much to convince her she was. Maybe a dive bar like this, my element, not hers, would help see reality. Because where I wanted to take her was a darker. Darker than a bright, shiny soul like hers should ever be exposed to.

I flipped the lock and she let go of the breath.

We got out, and she smoothed her clothes again, then headed for the big metal door.

"Don't get into any trouble in the twelve seconds I leave you alone." I leaned against the car and smiled at her. God, she was so sexy and seductive. I'd have to be on my toes tonight to keep all the yahoos in a place like this away from her.

"I can take care of myself." She strutted across the parking lot to the front door and walked in.

"I'd like very much to see you do exactly that, love." I counted to ten before I followed.

She sat down at the bar, and a waitress looked her up and down. Yeah. Angel was way too shiny and bright to be in a place like this.

She didn't get a drink, and it only took me a second to flag the woman down and order one for her. I gave her an extra hundred bucks to deliver it right away. She did and pointed to me when Angel looked around to see who'd bought it for her.

I sauntered up to the bar and set my drink down, letting every man in the place know she was mine. "You're supposed to drop the whiskey into the beer, Angel."

"Oh, well, you know, cosmos are more my style." She looked anywhere but at me and smiled in a friendly go-away way.

She did not understand how to be in a place like this. We were so far below her paygrade it almost wasn't funny. "This isn't a pink drink kind of place."

It was adorable how she was trying to get rid of me and at the same time, angling her body toward mine. I leaned against her part of the bar and took a sip of her beer, further staking my claim on her.

Between her teeth she asked, "What are you doing over here, anyway?"

She honestly didn't realize. Didn't get it.

Why would she? Our relationship was professional when it needed to be, but I'd say we'd become friends.

Time to be more.

"I'm hitting on you." I lowered my voice, and it came out as a husky invitation that makes a girl's panties wet for me.

Apparently not hers. She whispered out of the side of her mouth, "You're going to scare off the other guys."

"Who?" I glanced right and left.

"Him." She motioned to the bar. Two swivel stools down sat potential one-night stand candidate number one, beer gut and a wife beater.

No way. She couldn't drink enough watery beer to want to do that guy.

Moving on to bachelor-not number two, desperation in a business suit. "Or him."

He was likely here cheating on his wife. She didn't want him.

Angel tilted her head toward the bartender. I shook my head this time. The guy actually had potential. Not bad looking, not a drunk, and he'd already made eyes at her. We were leaving. "Let's get out of here and do something fun to celebrate your freedom."

"I am going to have fun. Sex is fun."

The way she said it left no doubt in my mind she had no idea that it could be a helluva a lot of fun. Fucking Sparky.

"So, this is about the sex."

A beautiful blush spread across her cheeks. I'd like to see where else I could spread that flush too.

She watched the bartender, and avoided looking me in the eye, preparing for her lie. "No."

Uh-huh. I leaned in close and whispered so softly in her ear, letting my breath heat her up first. "You're a horrible liar."

Liar, liar, pants seriously on fire, and that fire lit up her skin down to her cleavage. Ah. That's what I liked to see.

"I am not." She was trying so hard to be tough and confident.

I loved it and didn't back off an inch. "If this isn't about sex, why did your chest and neck flush?"

She swallowed hard. "It's the alcohol. Plus, why are you looking at my chest anyway?"

"There isn't a man in here who isn't." I raised my eyes back up to her. "And you've only had about a half a sip of that whiskey and even less of the beer, so good try."

She grabbed the shot glass, downed the rest, and slammed it on the table. "Fine. It's about the sex."

The surrounding tables went quiet, and we got several knowing looks. I didn't care. I'd gotten her to admit what she wanted.

What I could give her.

She lowered her voice for this go around. "So, what if it is? I'm entitled to spread my wings, or in this case my legs, if I want to. If I want a one-night stand and to have sheet-sweaty, shouting sex, I'm going to have it. I'm not engaged anymore. I can have dirty, dirty sexcapades with anyone I want."

I nodded and my eyes flicked down to her chest and back up in a nice slow perusal. "Yes, you can. It's about time, too."

"What's that supposed to mean?"

I chuckled. "Just that I doubt Sparky was very imaginative in the sack."

She swallowed and avoided my eye. "I have no response to that."

Because the only correct comeback would have been duh.

It had been a long time since I'd pursued any woman. I didn't want any other ones besides her. Time to take it up a notch. "What turns you on, Angel?"

A shiver floated across her skin. "I'm not talking about this with you."

"If you really want to get your rocks off, this isn't the place to do it." Which was half the reason I let her come in here.

"You've got someplace better?" She sipped her beer and looked around the dank bar. Anyplace was better than here.

"Yes." The carriage house, or the back of the limo, or her room, or on one of my motorcycles. None of those were where I was about to suggest. They were intimate. She needed down and dirty.

I needed to give that to her.

"Where?"

"Ever heard of The Asylum?"

"The BDSM sex club?"

My innocent little Angel knew more than I thought.

"We can't go there. It's members only, and I've heard it's practically impossible to be considered unless you are sponsored by another member. Money can't even buy its way in. It's harder to get in than the country club."

I listened, nodding, agreeing with her report. "I can get you in."

She looked surprised. What did I expect? She'd let me into her life, but I hadn't let her into mine. She had no way of knowing.

My world was dark and dangerous.

"How?" There was definite interest in her voice.

"I'm a member."

Sweet Angel almost fell off of her chair.

Perfect. I'd need her off balance, because I was about to take her into the lion's den and hoped she both survived and didn't hate me tomorrow.

NEW FUCKING FRIENDS

"*Y*ou're real funny. The Asylum. I'm so sure. Like I would fit in there." She slugged me in the arm.

Not the reaction I was looking for.

I didn't move a millimeter. "I'm not kidding."

"Sure. Right. Thanks for trying, but I'm telling you the only thing that will cheer me up is sending Marc dirty pictures of me in bed with another man."

Fuck. I just got shut down. She was back to her stupid revenge sex with a stranger plan.

God damn it.

I waited a beat, huffed out a quick breath, and frowned at her. "How exactly do you propose to take said pictures?"

"Uh, I guess it'll have to be a selfie?"

"Have you thought any of this so-called plan through? Like where do you plan to do the deed and how are you going to get rid of him when you're done?"

This was not only a security nightmare, and her safety was my number one priority, but there was no way I was letting her go through with revenge sex with a complete stranger.

"I don't know. I don't have to know. You think every woman who has ever had a one-night stand pre-planned everything?"

Time to get all protective and do my fucking job. "You're not taking some random guy back to the brownstone."

She fucking shrugged me off. "Okay, safety police, I'll suggest we go to his place."

"Because that won't get you murdered or worse," I growled.

She threw up her hands, getting frustrated. "What do you want from me?"

A lot more than she wanted to give me. "For you to get your head out of your ass."

I should have known better than to run my mouth like that at her. She had enough men in her life insulting her.

"Go away."

Not a chance. "Why, because you know I'm right?"

"No, because I don't care if you are. I'm doing this with or without your help." She shoved me and this time I let her think she could make me move.

Jesus, I knew that face. Normally, it was fun watching when she decided she was going to go after something she wanted. There was no stopping her. Not even I could stand in her way.

Fuck a duck.

"Fine. But I will be right over there watching every move every man makes on you, and if for one minute I think you're not safe, I'm hauling your ass out of here."

I wouldn't let any man do more than buy her a drink and talk to her for about five minutes. Yeah, I was that asshole.

I headed back toward my spot near the door where I could see the majority of the bar in one glance.

Angel stuck her tongue out at me.

There were so many other things I'd rather she did with that tongue. "I saw that."

"You did not."

I pointed to the mirror behind the bar and kept walking. She did it again.

I forced a smile, then narrowed my eyes in the you-better-behave look. I used to be a lot better at that.

She looked around the place again and indicated toward several dodgy looking dudes. I shook my head at each and every one.

Might as well go home, love.

Or let me take you somewhere better.

My mental telepathy worked. Or my scowls at all of her choices of men did, because she pushed the beer away and stood. Good. She was ready to go.

To where, we'd see.

Three steps across the room and she stopped short, staring.

Damn it. Where had those two guys come from? They made their way through the crowd and Angel's eyes followed them.

A burn, the same feeling as when I'd been shot, only from the inside, bloomed across my chest.

I'd lost her.

She was never mine, but now, she would be someone else's.

I couldn't let that happen.

If I didn't, I wasn't any better than her father and Marc. They'd done everything to control her life.

She deserved a chance to find out who she was on her own.

I should walk away.

I couldn't.

She was mine.

She'd never be mine until let her find her own way in the world first.

It was going to kill me.

She laughed, and she pushed a strand of hair behind her ear, shyly flirting with them. These two gigolos couldn't believe their luck.

I watched her with them. Two minutes in the company of men who wanted to fuck her, and her adorkable confidence was already soaring.

There was nothing hotter than a woman who knew what she wanted.

Could I be man enough to give it to her?

If I wanted to stay in her life, I had to give her everything.

Okay. New plan.

I could do this. I could share Angel. Even the thought of if it made my insides feel like a swamp in the desert.

Different mindset. Make it work.

Angel was mine.

Which meant... I was her Dom. I had no doubt she would be a beautiful submissive. My submissive.

I didn't play green subs. They had to have experience if they wanted me to handle their needs.

Just like that last girl I'd played back at the Asylum hadn't been ready for the likes of me, neither would Angel be.

This was like any other training. She would learn her limits. I'd be there to push them, because while I might share her for the time being, she was still under my protection.

I absolutely would be in control of this situation, this training.

I grabbed a bottle of water from the waitress and made my way over to their table. If Angel wanted to play, she would also learn about being safe, sane, and consensual. That meant no more alcohol.

"Hey, Angel. Who are your new friends?" I set the water in front of her, swung a chair around to the table, plopped down into it, and slung my arm around her shoulders.

She tensed right up.

"Go away," She whispered between her teeth and smiled at the men who would begin her training.

"Hey, man, we didn't realize she was here with someone." The taller man raised his hands and sat back in his chair. The other one pushed back from the table.

"She is." My grip on her shoulder tightened. Here goes. "But that doesn't mean she can't have some fun."

The two men glanced at each other. Angel darted away from me and out from under my arm.

The shorter guy shook his head. "If you two are doing some sort of revenge sex fight game, we do not want to get in the middle of that."

Angel held up her hands. "No, no. It's nothing like that. I swear."

This should be interesting to see how she handled this situation.

"What's it like then?" he asked.

I grabbed the beer nearest me and took a swig, acting

casual, so Angel wouldn't realize there was a volatile fire sparking right in front of her. I rubbed her arm, petting her. "Angel here wants to sow her wild oats."

The tall man frowned and narrowed his eyes. "And you're just going to let her?"

Like it was the most commonplace thing in the world, I said, "I'm going to watch."

TAKE CHARGE OR LOSE HER

These two guys, Hawk and Ian, weren't stupid. They were definitely in the lifestyle, and I'd check with Jackass later to see if they were members of The Asylum.

If they weren't, I'd make them a deal they couldn't refuse to walk away from Angel after tonight.

They smartly assessed the situation and agreed to my terms for a night with Angel between them.

My loft at Cruz towers. I maintained total control.

Gut instinct told me Ian was a switch, but it rankled Hawk to let someone else be in charge. He would though, if he wanted to play.

And he wanted to. He couldn't take his eyes off Angelina.

We walked outside to the waiting limo. She waved Ian and Hawk into the car ahead of us. Before she could follow, I grabbed her elbow and held her back from the open door. "Are you sure you want to do this, Angel?"

God how I wanted her to say no.

She needed to say yes.

I knew she did.

"You know I do. If I can't get back at Marc by sleeping with the help, then why not two men who will do everything to me he wouldn't?"

I was the help, and I wouldn't sleep with her.

She was going to make me regret that for a long time. It was the right choice.

I stepped closer, right in her personal space, looked down at her, scanning her face. She did her best to hold her ground. This was the new and improved Angel. The one who didn't cower in the face of imposing men. Already changing before my eyes.

It was time for her to learn who was in charge now. I narrowed of his eyes and clenched my jaw to keep from telling her to get down on her knees right here and right now for me.

She'd be following my commands soon enough.

We climbed into the limo and I took up a position across from her, making sure she knew I was watching every move.

She was no skilled courtesan, which these men figured out when she interpreted getting to know each other into fucking her.

With a stern look from me, Hawk slowed her down.

"How are you at sucking cock, doll?"

Angel glanced at me and I was very careful to display no reaction. She didn't like that.

She didn't respond to me, but gave her lovers for the night some back talk.

Lesson one. I don't lose my control.

"On your knees, Angel." My voice, dark and smoky, pushed at her submission. I commanded the space now.

Indecision warred on her face. She didn't yet know if I was

in her head, if I knew she was having some trepidation over showing these men her body and her submission.

I wanted to see her there.

"You're a naughty thing. I can't decide if your boyfriend there likes it or not." Hawk nodded to me. "But I don't, so get your mouth over here and start sucking my cock." He grabbed her head and pulled it to him.

The blood rushed through my body, and it took every fucking bit of training and willpower I had not to catapult myself across the limo and kill the son of bitch as he pushed his cock past her lips and all the way to the back of her mouth.

She gagged, and he held her there, thrusting deeper until she couldn't breathe. The car hit a bump in the road shoving him into her throat.

"Fuck, yeah. Take it deep, swallow me."

She wrenched her head back and gasped for air.

Hawk's hands didn't leave her head. "You like it a little rough, don't you, doll?"

Angel's nod soothed the beast in me that wanted to kill these men.

She was turned on. If I got my own head out of my ass I could see that.

She was gulping in breath and wiping at her mouth. I'd bet every penny I'd earned in the past three years that she was already wet.

Hawk indicated to Ian, who unbuckled his pants. "Suck him and use your tongue like you were on me. I want you to blow his mind."

It's exactly what I would have said if I wasn't dumbstruck by wanting her mouth on my own cock.

"Hang on a second." Angel grabbed her bag, pulled out her

phone and flicked the screen to video. "Would you mind filming this?"

She handed the phone to me.

Fucking hell. Was she doing this to torture me?

No. She had no idea my control was shattering.

"You are a dirty girl. What are you going to do with such an incriminating item?" Ian asked.

Two men, on a tape, delivered to Marc? Ultimate payback. "Revenge."

"I knew it," Ian said, his voice hinting that the idea turned him on. "Who are we getting revenge on?"

"Nobody important."

Not anymore.

The guys exchanged a look that said they thought we were crazy and decided they didn't care as long as they were getting laid.

What dude wouldn't when they had a sexy, curvy woman like Angelina between them?

Look what I was willing to endure for her.

"Gray? Will you film us for me?"

Now or never. I either took the phone and made this scene memorable for her or I kicked these dudes out of the car and fucked her myself.

I leaned forward in the seat, coming out of the darkness.

"You can watch like you love to do and film us. That way we can use it again later." She acted the role I'd invented at the bar, hoping I wouldn't back out now.

Her face begged me to play along.

I took the fucking phone, pointed it at her, and spoke to the guys.

Lesson two. I was in charge. Always.

"Take it up a notch. Get her good and ready for when we get to my place. But don't penetrate anything else besides her mouth until we're there. I want her worked up and ready to beg for it."

Arms wrapped around her and the men did everything I wanted to do to her.

Angel groaned and peered over at me. "Are you getting this?"

Could she see how much I cared that they had their hands all over her? I wasn't immune to it all.

"Are you getting off on it?" I kept my face hidden behind the light, and my voice flat, bland, like I didn't care about anything more than her safety and getting the shot. Like a porno director.

Hawk knelt on the floor of the car next to her and lowered his head to her breast. He sucked her flesh into his mouth, working her fast and hard. Ian played with the other breast pulling and tugging, tightening her skin into a hard peak.

They were just getting started, and I didn't know how much more I could take.

"Mmm-hmm." She finally answered my question with a moan.

"Then don't worry about it. We'll get your dirty sex tape made and then some."

Hawk grabbed her breasts, pushing them together. "Christ, yes. But you're not getting out of your part, Ian. Push that skirt up and her panties down. You were instructed to get her ready to beg. Finger her while I fuck her tits."

The steel in my voice broke through my hazy excitement. "Leave the panties on. She'll be sensitive enough through them."

The guys paused for half a breath. The power of my command hung in the air. Ian answered. "Yes, sir."

A shiver rolled over Angel's entire body. Yes, she wanted to be fingered. Yes, she wanted to lick that big dick before it slid across her cleavage. But those weren't the cause of her sudden quivers. It was the domination in my voice and the immediate submission in Ian's.

She loved it.

Finally, something I could give her.

This time my authority was directed at her. "And you, Angel. Don't even think about coming. You come when I say you can. Do you understand?"

She whimpered, and took several breaths and gulps, trying to stave back the orgasm that was so close.

Her submission was beautiful.

When we were on our own, I'd make her say it out loud. I'd make her tell me she wasn't allowed to come, say it over and over.

Until she was begging me to make her.

"Straddle me, babe. Put those big titties right in my face."

Angel froze, and an old insecurity surfaced. I'd seen it a million times with her. She was worried about her body and her weight.

The light from the phone flicked off. I figured it would help her get through this moment if I wasn't filming it.

I leaned in close, pushing Hawk and Ian back. "Don't think. If you start thinking, you'll get way too far into that head of yours. Just feel. Experience."

She blinked and breathed in, doing her best to follow that order too.

The guys knew what they were doing and didn't give her

long enough to reconsider before they started using her like some human sex toy to increase the fun and pleasure of a blow job. Angelina moaned and whimpered and was definitely turned on by it.

They fucked her body without being inside of her, using her tits and her cleft.

I wanted her close to coming, wanting her ready to beg.

She gasped and her legs trembled. Fuck me, she was there.

"Yes, please. Please."

The car came to a screeching stop, just as I had texted the driver to do when he got to Cruz Towers. Couldn't have been better timing.

Nobody was coming tonight without my say so.

The three of them tumbled into the seats and each other. Face down in the carpet was no place for a good time. Now, vice versa was another story.

"What the fuck, man?" Hawk shouted toward the front seat.

I shoved her phone into my pocket and said, "We're here."

I looked Angel in the face, needing a minute alone with her, barely trusting myself to have it.

Hawk lifted her off of Ian and moved her to the seat. I heard them clear their throats, and then they get out of the car.

Angel and I couldn't move or look away from each other.

When they were gone and it was only the two of us, then I let my gaze roam, and plunder her body. She was naked from her stomach up and her skirt bunched around her waist. She was so damn tempting.

"You're fucking gorgeous like this, on edge and shameless."

I was well beyond turned on by her and at the edge of my control.

I needed her.

Now.

GET IT TOGETHER

*I*f I took Angelina now, I could have her for only that one moment in time.

She would submit to me. Of course she would. But just this once. Just this time. Because tonight was about her learning about pleasure for the first time.

It would set her on a path into my sinful, wicked, dark world.

I could either have her now at the beginning and she would quickly outgrow me, or I could have her when she came into her own, became the women she was meant to be, a confident, sexual being who would have me bowing at her feet.

Both choices scared the shit out of me.

What if she wouldn't have me? She'd already rejected me once tonight.

No. I would not lose her for good for a moment of divine pleasure with her.

She would know I wanted her.

"I hated every second of those two having their hands on

you, and I thought I would destroy the damn car when that tall bastard wanted to come on your face."

I enjoyed every second of staring at her. I hated that enjoyment.

I didn't want to want her. Not like this.

Not until she could want me back.

"I'll give you a minute to put yourself back together. If you'd like something else to wear once we're up there, I can arrange for that. But you can also go naked." He clenched my jaw. "It's your choice."

It was her choice. Yes or no, pretty Angel. Will you have me now or later?

I couldn't bring myself to let her have that power yet.

She scowled at me. "Hurt much to say that?"

I could take anything but her lashes at me.

That's what broke my control.

"Damn it. Don't fucking push me away like one of your country club dickheads. I know what I'm doing here. You need this," I pointed out the car door toward the guys and the front of the building, "more than my need to protect you or fuck you. So, pull yourself together and go in there and get your brains screwed out."

She pulled back, shocked that I'd yelled at her.

"You don't really want me to do this, do you?"

I'd gone along with the idea to go to that bar, and I'd agreed to make the sexy tape for her. I'd hated every one of her requests all night, tried my best to get in the way.

Because I had feelings for her.

She wasn't some piece of ass. She wasn't another sub for me to fuck.

I sighed and ran a hand through my hair. "What I want

doesn't matter right now. You need this. You've never gotten a chance to be you, now you can find out who you are and what you like. If this is what you like, well..."

Those were the first honest words to come out of my mouth all night.

She raised her face so I saw every expression, every sincerity written there. She wanted the truth from me.

"Why can't I do that with you?"

God, how I wanted that.

But at what cost?

I was a fucking coward.

I took her jaw in my hands and brushed my lips across hers for the first time. It was nothing like any kiss I'd ever experienced.

The taste of warmth and compassion, love and lust seeped into my mouth. I needed this woman. The realization was like when you were looking for something right in front of you.

I needed and wanted Angel on a level way beyond friendship, Domination and submission, and even beyond sex. She saw me when no one else did.

I stared down at her, searching my eyes. Neither of us were ready for where this relationship would take us. So, I'd be the asshole one more time. I'd break this tenuous thread of vulnerability between us. Because if I didn't, she wouldn't get out of this car and she wouldn't go upstairs with anyone but me.

She needed to become her own woman.

If I didn't break her in the process, I'd be there when she was ready to take over the world.

But I had to hurt her, just like her fucktard of a fiancé did. It was the only way.

I said the words bound to make her forget about being with me.

"I won't be your rebound."

Now, who was the douchebag?

Me. That's who.

COME, FOR ME

My plan worked too well.

Angel was pissed at me once again.

Fine. I needed a minute to get my shit together.

I was falling in love with Angelina Cruz. A woman so out of my league, she didn't even imagine there was a league.

When we all got up to my apartment, I told Hawk to fuck her. It's what she needed.

I excused myself and hurried into my office. There on the security monitors, they were already taking her back to that place of bliss they'd found in the limo.

They still knew better than to make her come without my say so.

I hit record. If Angel wanted a revenge sex tape, I'd make a fucking art piece out of her. Sparky did not know what he was missing.

My reflection stared back at me in the light of the monitors.

"Get your shit together, man."

I watched and listened. They talked about Angel's real motivations, and I was rapt with what she'd say about me.

"Don't lie to me," Hawk said.

Like she even knew how.

"I'm not. This is definitely revenge, but not on Gray. He isn't even my boyfriend."

No. I wasn't. I was no mere boy, and she and I were no longer friends. I didn't know what we were.

"What is he then?" Hawk's eyebrows lowered, ready to furrow if he found the wrong answer.

She shook her head.

How the fuck should she know? This whole night, we'd been something more than our regular relationship ever even hinted at.

"Believe me when I say I don't know right now."

The answer mostly satisfied them. They were decent guys, even if they were dirty fuckers. Different from most of the guys in the lifestyle. Like Bennett.

Hawk and Ian began undressing her, and I headed back to the living room. She could be mad at me all she wanted, but she was still mine. I'd gotten my control back in the couple of minutes away.

They could fuck her. But her orgasm was mine.

Ian was balls deep inside of her when I returned. I pretended like hell that didn't matter to me.

"That's right, doll. Jesus, you're a beautiful fuck."

He was right. She'd be even more gorgeous when I finally let her come.

"Shit, her pussy is gripping me like a fat fist." Ian groaned and pulled out of her. Hawk's fingers pressed tight against her clit but stopped moving.

She thrust her hips forward, searching for more of the pleasure. "No, don't stop. Please. I need to come."

"I know," Ian said.

Hawk flicked her skin in whisper-light strokes that were nowhere near enough to do anything besides drive her crazy. "But you don't get to come. Remember, naughty girl?"

"Ever?"

"Not until I say," I said.

"Please," she whispered.

Her words rushed through my body like the aphrodisiac they were, making my cock harder than it had been all night.

Their three bodies stilled, waiting for my command. "Not yet. You're not ready."

Hawk smiled at that. He was as sadistic as I was. They fucked her, with their cocks and fingers, bringing her to the edge and back again.

I gripped the side of the marble counter top so hard my knuckles were white.

I wanted to shout for them to make her come.

Not yet.

"Please, Hawk, please."

She hadn't begged me, asked for my permission. She'd learn that third lesson soon enough.

"That's it. Good girl. Such a hot mouth. You're getting me all kinds of hard. I can't wait to fuck you."

She pulled her mouth away from his fingers. "Then fuck me."

"You don't understand what you're asking. My pleasures run darker than Ian's. I want your ass, doll." He pressed against her pushing his hard cock against the back of her thighs.

My mind swirled with visions of fucking Angel's tight ass for myself. I doubted if anyone had ever taken her there before.

The forbidden and taboo idea almost pushed me into orgasm. I shuddered and sucked in a shattered breath.

"Ian?"

"Yeah, babe?" His voice was shaky and his eyes closed. He was holding back from coming too. I wondered if that was part of their game.

No more games.

"I want Hawk's dick in me, too. I want both of you. Can we do that?"

Jesus Christ, superstar. My Angel was going to get everything she needed and more tonight.

Fuck me, she was hot.

"Fuck, yeah, we can. I wasn't sure we'd get to tonight. Are you sure? You know what you're asking?"

She was asking for a sexual experience to obliterate every lacking, orgasmless, missionary, vanilla thing she'd ever done in her life. "Yes, I want this. I need it."

Hawk searched her for consent too. "You're sure this is what you want? We don't have to. I get almost as much out of controlling the scene as I do fucking you."

Welcome to my world, love.

"Yes. I've wanted to do this for a long time."

She had? How long?

Why didn't I know this?

Hawk nodded and rubbed his thumb over her mouth. "Good."

He glanced over to me, asking one last time to give her

what she needed. I nodded. It was high time everyone got to fucking come.

"Then your punishment is over. I think it's time we heard you scream."

They positioned Angelina so she was straddling Ian and bent her forward so Hawk could fuck her ass from behind.

They might be the lucky bastards inside of her, but each of their movements were mine. I imagined it was my cock bringing her pleasure. My cock positioned at the tight ring of her ass.

From her new perspective, she could see past Ian and into the kitchen where I stood, leaning casually.

I couldn't look away. I had to watch, torturing both of us. I'd seen more of her tonight than ever. Not just her body, but her desires, her vulnerability, her pleasure.

She whispered my name. The moment the sound left her lips, I pushed against the wall and stood, filling the doorway, the room with my presence.

They fucked her with their fingers, getting her ready. God, how I wanted to give her the first real taste of this illicit act.

Every cell in my body was aware of her, on high alert. My muscles were tensed, my breathing rapid, like I was ready for a fight.

Our eyes locked. She mouthed her need for me. Me. "Fuck me."

Shit. How I wanted to take her, claim her. But I shook my head.

More than ever before, we both knew she needed more time to explore her own sexuality.

If I wouldn't fuck her, I'd have to watch while someone else did. While I imagined I was inside of her.

"Are you ready, doll?"

She stared right at me, taunting me with her body and her words. "I'm more than ready. Take me."

She never once took my eyes off of my face. From behind my back, I raised her phone, filming everything for her. For me.

This was the dirtiest, filthiest thing she'd ever done, and she loved every second. If that was true, maybe I could take her even darker places. Just her and me.

Hawk slid into her ass and with a slow rhythm, being gentle, he fucked her. It took a minute for Ian to catch up, but soon his cock matched the pace, sliding in and out of her body.

She wasn't even aware of the soft keen of pleasure coming out of her mouth. The camera faltered my hands, so set the camera on the counter, propped against a bottle of water and still aimed at her.

I'd done this a hundred times, thinking of her. Now, I'd let her see exactly how fucking much I wanted her, needed her.

I unbuckled my pants and let them hang open. I never wore underwear, preferring commando. My pants didn't have to drop far before my cock poked out the top. I gripped it in one hand and stroked down to the base.

Angel watched me touch myself and sucked in a hiss of breath when I played with the shiny mental balls of the piercings. Yes, that's right baby, a little pain, a whole lot of pleasure.

My imagination ran wild and crazy at the thought of feeling my metal inside of her, pumping like Ian and Hawk.

"Fuck, honey, that's right. Come for me. Fuck, fuck, fuck," Hawk chanted and increased his pace. Ian had become incoherent, a long, broken moan coming from deep in his chest.

"Come for me. Let me hear you scream. Come on, I'm fucking close. Fuck. I'm going to fill your ass." Hawk thrust hard, Ian pumped into her, and she reached her arm out for me.

My hand sped over my cock. My mouth moved, forming words even I couldn't hear, but she didn't need to. She knew exactly what I was saying. "Come for me, Angel. Come now."

She screamed, my name on her lips. My entire body, my whole world collapsed, and the stars I'd been seeing with each of the guy's thrusts into her exploded into a giant super nova.

"Angel."

MINE

*H*awk lifted Angel under the legs and behind her back.

"You got a bed and a bathroom in this place, man?" Hawk walked toward me.

"Right down the hall, on the left."

I leaned against the wall, trying my best to appear like I'd been watching a game of checkers instead of jerking off to Angel's foray into the wild side.

Why did I have the feeling she could see right through me?

I gave them a minute and Ian, who was still laying on the couch, said something.

"Sorry. What?"

He uncovered the arm over his face.

"You don't know what you're missing, dude."

"I do."

"Then what the hell are you standing here for? Go fucking take her, before Hawk tries to steal her away."

Shit.

I walked back toward the bedroom and overheard precisely what Ian had warned me of.

"I don't suppose I could steal you away from your boy—" he paused, obviously remembering Angel's reprimand from earlier about what we were to each other, "from Gray?"

Time for them to get the fuck out.

"Thank you for tucking her in. I can take it from here." I'd pulled myself back together, so Hawk didn't see how the way he'd fucked my girl had affected me.

Angel kissed Hawk softly on the lips and whispered, "I'm not his to steal from, but still."

"Yeah, I didn't think so."

I cleared my throat and crossed the room. "I've got a car waiting downstairs for you."

"Well, that's my wham bam thank you ma'am cue to get out of here, doll. I'll leave my card on the kitchen counter. Call me if you want to do this again... or if you don't and just want to get away from your Neanderthal."

He returned her kiss, sneaking his tongue across her lips. She smiled, but didn't let him in.

That's my girl.

I expected she'd want to talk about what had happened here tonight or at least yell at me for being such a complete bonehead.

Instead, she fell asleep.

I made sure the guys left, then I slowly shed my clothes. I folded hers and laid them on the chair for her to find in the morning. All except her frilly little panties.

Those were mine now.

I hid them away in the nightstand's drawer, imagining wrapping them around my cock later. Coming in them.

I was painfully hard again just having her naked body next to me.

My days in Delta had taught me to be a light sleeper, and from years of protecting her, I knew she was a deep one.

I could indulge, hold her lush curves close to my hard angles for a few hours, and she'd never need to know because I'd be up long before she was.

It was a shitty way to have a relationship. At the moment, we didn't even have that. We didn't know what we were to each other.

For a little while, I could pretend she was mine.

It would take time for her to throw off all the old fears and negative core beliefs that had been ground into her, but having crazy-ass ménage sex, on film, was a damn good way to start.

The next morning, she found me in the kitchen making breakfast. She sat down at the counter and watched me. She hadn't made a sound, but I knew she was there and slid a cup of sweet and creamy coffee in front of her.

"We should—" She began the morning after speech about having to talk about it, but I cut her off by a spatula held up like a stop sign.

"We'll talk. But after you eat." I pulled two plates out of the oven and plopped eggs onto them, followed by *chicharrons*. One plate I set down for her and the other at the next seat over.

Her stomach growled, and for once, she didn't say no to food. We tucked in and she snuck glances at me, waiting for the right moment.

"Gray—" she started again, only to be cut off by my finger on her lips.

"Angel, look. You were amazing last night. It killed me, but you were so damn perfect in your exploration. I hope you got what you were looking for."

"I think I did."

"Good. You should continue to explore what you want from life, from men."

"I've been thinking a lot about that. About you."

"I know. But when you come to me, I want you to be you. The real you. Not the Stepford Barbie rich bitch, but the smart, savvy, sexual woman you were meant to be."

"I'm not any of those things."

"You've never given yourself a chance to be."

I was challenging us both.

"I am changing, discovering what I want and what I don't. But I already know I want you in my life."

In her bed. She left that part unsaid.

We both knew I would be there someday.

I reached for her face, but withdrew my touch. Had I screwed this up too badly to be more than a man she fucked? "I can't be what you want."

She'd gone so far to letting me see the real her. Yet, here I was hiding from her. I'd made a lot of excuses last night why we couldn't be together. I had even more this morning.

She held my hand and kissed the inside of my wrist. It was such an intimate gesture, and it took my breath away.

"Maybe not yet, and maybe we need some time to figure out the next step. We don't have to be in a hurry."

She set down her fork and slipped off the barstool. A few minutes later she reappeared wearing a shirt and sweater of mine.

That was so fucking sexy.

We rode down the elevator in silence, but I couldn't help standing closer to her than usual, touching her in little casual ways. When we walked out and through the lobby, I placed my hand on the small of her back guiding her, protecting her.

In the garage, I took her hand and helped her into a town car. No driver today. I would drive her home this morning. Get her all to myself for a little while longer.

ONLY THE GOOD DIE YOUNG

*A*ngel's phone rang, and she it answered on the car's speaker without even looking to see who was on the other end of the line.

I'd taught her better than that. This time I wasn't sad to get to listen in on this conversation.

"Angie, please, let's talk about this."

Marc. I'd recognize his whiny voice anywhere, anytime.

"There's nothing to talk about, Sparky." He hated when I called him by the nickname. It would drive him insane to hear it from Angel now.

That's what he got for calling her Angie all these years. Angel suited her much better. She'd never been an Angie.

Rich white guys thought they owned the world, and that included all the women in it. What amazed me about Sparky was that Angel had a serious kink streak that would make most any man permanently hard at how fucking hot she was.

She'd implied she wanted to spice up their sex life, and it had disgusted him. Then he'd gone and fucked Mindy in the ass where anyone could have discovered them.

"If your shit isn't out of the house by the time I get home in, oh, a half an hour... I'm burning it."

Mmm. Cuddling up with her by a warm fire did sound nice.

"Where were you last night, Angie?"

"Not that it's any of your business, but I went out."

"All night? With who? I hope you had Grayson with you."

"Yes, I had Grayson."

But not the way I wanted her to.

"Ange, come home. Let's talk."

Not a chance. "Fuck you, Marc."

"Watch your language."

"I don't think so, asshole. Get out of my fucking house, stop dicking around with my friends, and go fucking fuck yourself."

I almost laughed out loud. We'd work on her cursing creativity.

"What in the hell has gotten into you?" Marc's whine was getting higher in pitch with each question.

"*Que te folle un pez.*" She pushed the button to hang up.

I heard her clicking on her phone and hoped she was blocking his number.

"Did I just hear you to tell Marc to get fucked by a fish?"

The smile that had been missing all morning from her face came back.

"Something like that," she laughed.

A few minutes later, my phone rang. Angel scooted forward to the front of the car and had to cover her mouth to keep from bursting out laughing.

I had the phone held away from my ear so we both heard that same damn whiny tone Marc used to yell.

I let it go on for about thirty seconds before I hung up on the bastard. "You really sent him a video of last night?"

"Yep."

"Good girl."

I loved saying those words to her. I'd love it even more when she was coming on my dick.

"Dirty, naughty, good girl."

"That I am."

It was fully time for her to embrace it. I would grit my teeth and bear it, but she had some rebounding to do.

"What's next, Angel?"

She slid back into the comfort of the seat and grinned at the world, at Marc, at me. "Take me home. But tonight, we're going out again."

I chuckled. "Oh, fuck. I've created a monster in you, haven't I? A succubus, or Aphrodite, I'm not sure which."

"And Gray?"

I glanced at her in the rearview mirror and she looked like I was about to pounce on me. As fun as that might have been, not yet.

"I want you to take me to The Asylum."

Aw, shit. I shook my head, the smile fading. "I don't know about that."

"I do. I've been a goody-goody doing what daddy said until the past two days, and really it was no life at all. I'm done with that."

Only the good die young, and she wanted to live.

I wanted to let her. Even if it killed me. I would revel in her journey, even if I couldn't claim her body.

She glanced at me, and I didn't quite interpret what this

look meant. All I knew now was that this gorgeous curvy woman had changed my life, taken it from dark desperation. I was thoroughly taken with her. Entirely seduced.

THIS SPECIAL PRINT edition of Revel also includes the short epilogue Christmas story, *Rejoice* which takes place after the *Curvy Seduction Saga*. Turn the page for more of Gray and Angelina's sexy adventures.

REJOICE

REJOICE

Angelina:
Gray hates Christmas. How did I not know this?
I lurve the holidays.
I'm going to unscrooge him.
*rubs hands together and starts planning

Gray:
Best way to spend Christmas?
In bed. With Angel under me. Begging me.
Sucking me like a candy cane.
Screw the holidays.

"...I am as happy as an angel..."

—Ebenezer Scrooge, *A Christmas Carol* by Charles Dickens

THE PLAN

a private island in the tropics. Check.
A super-hot guy who brings me cold drinks. Check.

A candy cane striped vibrator I hoped said hot guy would use on me come Christmas morning wrapped and under the palm tree I'd strung with lights and tinsel. Check.

I was so ready for the holidays.

"Angel, my love." Gray squirted a handful of sunscreen into his palm and started in on my shoulders. I was eager for him to rub that lotion quite a bit lower. "How about we skip Christmas this year?"

I rolled over and sat up. "Skip? Christmas? But I already got you a present."

"You don't have to get me anything. Being with you is present enough." He kissed me, soft at first, teasing me with promises of what else his lips and tongue could do. Those lotioned-up hands of his snuck inside my tankini top and pinched and pulled at my nipples.

Mmm. I wasn't the only one with skills. Gray used his for

distraction and it worked like a charm. I leaned into his touch and groaned, wanting more.

Wait a minute.

I broke the kiss. "You're trying to distract me. We are not canceling Christmas Mr. Scroogy McScrooge."

He rolled my hard flesh between his fingers and licked his lips. "Bah, humbug."

Mierda, he made me go all swoony with those lusty sparkles in his eyes.

"What if I fuck you so long and hard you forget what day it is?"

It's not like he hadn't done it before. But that was a Monday. Nobody likes Mondays anyway.

Not Christmas day though. This was the first time we would get to spend our first major holiday as a couple.

My mother loved Christmas time. She always had all our presents bought by Halloween and we'd decorate the tree after dinner on Thanksgiving. Plus, Christmas cookies were the bomb.

Even after she was gone and my father had wanted nothing to do with the holidays, Gray had celebrated plenty of Christmases with me, just never as my lover.

I didn't remember him having a humbug attitude about it before. I needed to get to the bottom of this.

I circled my arms around his neck and batted my eyelashes at him. "Yes. Let's do that. Right after Christmas."

He sighed. I hated it when he did that. It meant he was avoiding telling me something hidden deep inside that hot head.

"Hey. No more secrets, Gray. What's going on? Why don't you want to celebrate the holidays?"

His hands slid out of my top and that tic he got in his jaw pulsed. I hadn't seen that since we left the club behind. Bad sign.

The way to get him to relax and talk to me about what bothered him was well within my skill set. He was defenseless against the power of the boobs. Off went my swimsuit, and I pushed him back on his lounge chair, so I could straddle that luscious cock of his.

"Angel." Ooh, how I loved when he growled my name like that. "What do you think you're doing?"

There was an impressive bulge in his swim trunks that needed freeing. The laces came open easily and soon enough I wrapped my hands around him, stroking.

"Tell me what you've got against Christmas."

"This will not work, babe. You are not the one in charge here."

I swirled the bead of pre-cum from his tip and raised a smug eyebrow at him. "Talk and I'll make it worth your while."

"Fuck me and let me watch you come apart on my dick and I'll think about it."

A year ago, I lacked the confidence to be on top, much less ride a cock cowgirl style. Now, it was one of my favorite positions and Gray took advantage of that fact every chance he got.

It's not like I would say no to him, not when he enjoyed being ridden as much as I did.

I rose, and he grabbed his cock, sliding it into me as I sank down on to him. *Dios Mio*, there was nothing like the way he filled me.

Gray groaned and sunk his fingers into my hips, helping

me move up and down. "Fuck, I love being inside of you when you're so hot and wet like this. Ride me hard, Angel."

He was already thrusting and doing all the work. I was the one along for the ride now.

Maybe later I could make him talk. This was too good to mess with.

"Hand between your legs. I want to see you rub your clit for me. Show me how wet you are."

"Yes, sir."

His eyes grew even darker when I said those words. I didn't use them very often. Only when I wanted him to remember I was still his and his alone.

He pounded into me and it wouldn't take much more for me to explode. A few swipes of my fingers over my clit and I was already moaning his name.

"Gray, Gray, please, Gray. Please."

"Not yet, Angel. Don't you come until I tell you to. Do you understand?"

"Yes." Pant pant. I still sucked at orgasm control and he made me practice all the damn time. Sadistic bastard that I loved.

"Yes, what?"

Oh God. So close. "Yes." Mmm, I wasn't going to last much longer. "Sir."

"Not yet. Hands on your tits. Pinch your nipples nice and hard."

I whimpered but did as he said because we both liked it when I did. He didn't slow down for a second and surprised me when his hand pushed between us, stroking my clit with his thumb.

"Gray. *Por favor*. I can't. *Dios, por favor*."

"No. Your cunt is mine. Your orgasm is mine. You're mine."
Every one of his words dripped with lust and need.

"Yes, yes. I'm yours. Only yours."

"That's right. Are you allowed to come yet?"

He was driving me so high, so crazy. "No, sir."

"Good girl. Let me feel that cunt squeeze my cock nice and tight."

I swallowed and took short quick breaths just to concentrate on not coming while I tightened my inner muscles on him.

"Fuck, yes. That's it. You're so hot, baby. I love you so fucking much."

That was it. He could talk dirty to me all night and all day and it revved me right up. His talk of love lit me on fire for him. If he didn't let me come in the next ten seconds, I was going over the edge whether he wanted me to or not.

"Come for me, Angel."

"Yes, sir." The words barely crossed my lips before my pussy was spasming and my muscles locked, pulsing around him.

Gray called my name over and over and came with me, his hips jerking, his seed pushing deep inside of me.

When we were both sated, he pulled me down on top of him and cuddled me into his embrace. Softly, he stroked my hair as we floated in that blissful place together.

"It's not a big deal, baby. I've never liked Christmas. It's always been like any other day at work for me. But you have fun celebrating if you want. You don't have to worry about my bah-humbug interrupting your holiday."

That was so not the post-sexy times cuddle admission I was looking for.

Work schmerk. We had enough money neither of us ever needed to work ever again in our lives. He was being a Scrooge.

Fine. Then I would give him the three ghosts of Christmas treatment.

I stayed quiet and formed a plan in my head. When we got back to the casita, I had phone calls to make and some ghostly holiday fun to create.

PASSED THE PAST

A considerable amount of my fortune well spent, and I was ready for Christmas Eve eve. Also known as the Ghost of Christmas Past.

Gray would hate every second. I'd likely earn some serious spankings too. If it meant I could remind him just how miserable we'd both been before we were together, all the punishments he wanted to give me, would be worth it.

I'd sent Gray to the mainland to get groceries. He thought I planned to spread my version of holiday cheer with Christmas cookies. Ha.

My ghosts waited in the wings, ready to swoop in and help me transform the casita the second he was away.

"Angelina, are you sure you understand what you're doing? Gray will punch me in the face when he figures out what's going on here."

I so appreciated Jim coming down from the club two days before Christmas to be the official Ghost of Christmas Past. He'd even provided his own costume, in the form of combat fatigues and body armor.

"Trust me, Jim. He needs this."

I rearranged my wig again. God, this thing was itchy. I'd been a bleach bottle blonde engaged to one of the biggest assholes on Fifth avenue when this Christmas had gone down.

Full-sized cardboard cut-outs of said asshole and a bunch of my other high society ex-friends decorated the inside of the casita. The fake friends transformed our place into a replica of my country club at Christmas time.

Ew. Made me nauseated just thinking of those days.

"You're the boss. Who will be paying my cosmetic surgery bills to have my nose fixed when he's done with me?"

"You'll be fine. I'm the one who'll get my ass reddened if this doesn't work."

"That, I'd like to see." He waggled his eyebrows at me. Jim so needed to find himself a good sub. Dude had way too much sexual energy to be wasted on the flavor of the week.

"You're a perv." But such a sweet guy. Not that anyone would ever realize. He was too sexy and intimidating for his own good. I relished the day he met his match.

"Yep."

Tires crunched on the gravel driveway. Showtime.

"Angel?" Gray called from the front hallway. "Whose jeep is that outside?"

I skedaddled over to the pseudo country club bar and cued the elevator music and coffee shop talk track on the stereo. I sat on a barstool and pretended to drink my Cosmo. I even fake chatted with the cut-out of Mindy Monaghan of the Boston Monaghans.

I had my back to the entryway. Gray's presence filled the room the second he entered. He was silent for a minute, probably taking in my craziness.

"Jackass? What the hell is going on here? Angel?"

"Hey, man. Just remember she's doing all this for you, you dickhead." Jim cleared his throat and then woo-ed like a ghost. "Whoooooooooo."

"There is seriously something wrong with you." Gray groaned.

"Whooooooo. Grayson Scrooge, I am the Ghost of Christmas past. Whoooooo."

"Jesus Christ." The eye roll came out damn clear in Gray's voice. Please, please, please let him buy into this.

"No, that guy is the day after tomorrow," Jim deadpanned.

"Shut up and get on with your ghosting, Marley." Gray sounded resigned, but he wasn't putting a stop to this play.

I swallowed back the nervousness that bubbled up. I crossed my fingers Gray wouldn't blow this whole thing off.

"Whoooo. Come with me, Master Sergeant Grayson Scrooge to visit your Christmases past." Jim led Gray out of the room just like we'd planned.

That gave me plenty of time to stew about how mad he would be later.

The two of them returned in a half an hour. Gray wore his sand-covered fatigues now too. He definitely had his mad on.

"Fine. You want me to say I was fucking lonely sitting in that hellhole night after night. Then I'm saying it. Didn't matter if it was Christmas or not. Operators love their country and hate the military, especially on holidays."

Good thing Jim and Gray had been friends for a long time because anyone else might not have taken kindly to that dark mood getting fifty pounds of sand in pretend Iraq thrown at them created.

"Of course, you were. We all were. What I'm saying is you

weren't the only one lonely at Christmas, dickhead." Jim jerked his chin in my direction.

Gray glanced at me and then did a double take. I patted my hair and put on the fake smile I'd learned so well growing up.

"Hey, Gray." I'd rehearsed my lines a zillion times in the last half hour. Once again, I crossed my fingers he would play along. "Have you seen Marc? I can't find him anywhere."

Gray's eyes widened and then he frowned. He glanced around the room at the life-size cutouts of the people from my past.

I'd stashed Mindy behind the bar. No doubt with his training in observation, he noticed she was missing too.

Because he and I both knew exactly where Marc and Mindy were. I hadn't known back then.

Christmas a year ago, sitting at the country club surrounded by my so-called friends and family had been lonely. I'd insisted on hanging out at the bar waiting for my fiancé to show up. Grayson looking on, being the consummate bodyguard.

I was good at pretending that sitting there alone hadn't bothered me. How could it when there was so much holiday cheer to be had?

I was super at lying to myself about a lot of things back then.

Gray stared at me for a full minute. Without taking his eyes off of me, he addressed Jim. "Jackass, I'm sure there is a hot woman warming your bed at home. I got this."

Jim tipped his head to me and when I nodded, he saluted and walked out, grabbing the cut-out of the cute waitress on his way.

I worried my lip between my teeth as Gray crossed to me.

He lifted his hand to my face and ran his thumb across my mouth, stopping me from doing any more damage. "Why do I have the feeling there's a life-size cardboard replica of Sparky fucking Mindy in the bathroom?"

"Probably because there is."

He shook his head. "You went to a hell of a lot of trouble here. You didn't have to do this for me."

"I did too." Sometimes he was so dense.

"Okay, love." He grabbed a strand of my wig and rubbed it between his fingers. "I hope this isn't permanent. I never liked you blonde. The real you is so much more beautiful to me."

Sweet talker. I pulled the wig off and tugged my hair out of the tight bun. All along he'd seen more of the real me than anyone else ever had.

"Are you a little less scroogy now?"

"I never thought about you being lonely at Christmas. I'm sorry for that and I wish now I'd done something sooner. Come to bed with me now and I'll spend the whole night making it up to you."

He led me off toward our bedroom and I happily followed him.

He hadn't quite answered my question.

That was okay, because I had more in store for Gray. The Ghosts of Christmases Present and Future were on their way.

THE PRESENT

*P*hase two of Operation Unscrooge Gray was locked and loaded.

And by locked I meant my wrists in handcuffs around the base of the Christmas tree.

Yeah, yeah. I had the key within reach in case I had to pee or something before he woke up on Christmas morning and found me splayed out in my naughty Mrs. Claus costume for him.

My Ghost of Christmas Present was going to rock his world.

Just as soon as he discovered me.

Lucky for me he was an early riser. Gray sauntered in looking all delicious in the red satin fur-trimmed boxers I'd left out for him. Also... I may have hidden the rest of his clothes, so he had no other choice. Although, I would have taken him naked too.

"Well, well, well. Mrs. Claus, I presume." He stood over me with his arms crossed, but a twinkle in his eye.

"Nope. I'm your Ghost of Christmas Present."

"I do love a good present. I think I should wait to open my gift." He turned like he was headed to the kitchen.

"Don't you dare, Gray."

He kept walking.

"Grayson. Come back here and unwrap me." *Coño.*

He laughed. "Don't get your panties twisted. I'll be right there. I'm getting your present."

Aww. He got me a present.

Maybe he wasn't as scroogified as I'd thought.

He came back with two smallish boxes wrapped simply in red paper. The smaller gift was approximately the same size as one of my presents under the tree for him.

He sat down next to me on the floor. "I'm thoroughly enjoying seeing you cuffed, so I'll open these for you."

I smiled, and he ripped the wrapping off the smaller present. Inside was a velvet box. Ooh. Jewelry. Yay.

He flipped open the lid and diamonds sparkled back at me. At first, I thought they were earrings, but Gray pulled them out and dangled them closer so I could see.

They were clusters of fine jewels in the shape of angels and they weren't earrings at all. They were nipple clamps.

He knew the way to my heart - and my libido.

"Ooh. Put them on me, pretty please." I was more than ready to get these reindeer games started.

"Not yet, naughty Ghost of Christmas presents. I'll put them on you when I'm good and ready." He smacked the side of my butt to emphasize his point.

Meanie.

"It's Christmas Present."

He ignored me and tore the paper off the other box. From its depths came a red and white striped vibrator.

I laughed out loud.

"That is not the reaction I was expecting." Gray turned it on and positioned it right over my clit but didn't touch me. "It would be very easy for me to turn those giggles into groans and moans."

He brushed the fabric of the panties I had on and I laughed even harder. "Wait. Wait. Open that present. Right there, by my elbow."

"I'll open my presents once you've come a time or two." He pressed the vibrator against me and swirled it up and down my folds through the material.

"Gray. I got you the same thing."

He paused with the vibe a scant centimeter below my clit, just out of reach of where the sensations drove me crazy in all the best ways. His gaze flicked to the box I'd indicated and back to me.

I tried to wiggle so I could get the full effect of the toy, but he moved it every time I did. With his other hand he grabbed my be-ribboned gift and popped it open.

A matching candy cane vibrator came out of the box.

"You dirty girl. I've got plans for what to do with two of these and I doubt you'll be laughing with one in your pussy and the other in your sweet hot ass."

Uh-oh.

Gray set both the toys down and slid my panties from me and when they were off, threw them over his shoulder. "Spread your legs for me, love. Let me open my present now."

Dios Mio, I love Christmas.

I did as he demanded, and he laid on the floor, his face within licking distance. The buzz of one vibe started up again.

Gray ran it along the inside of my thigh, teasing me, making me wonder which way he would go with it.

Into my pussy it went, and he found exactly the right angle to hit my g-spot. A millisecond later his mouth was on my clit and he moved the vibrator in time with his licks and lashes of my nub.

"Oh, Gray. Fuck me."

He did.

Expertly.

Right before I was ready to come nice and hard, he lifted his head and pulled the toy out. "You taste like candy canes now."

"Don't stop." I didn't care if I tasted like the nectar of the gods.

"Don't stop what?" He raised an eyebrow at me.

My dirty bad boy always wanted to hear the words. If he wanted to torture me, I could tease him right back with my own version of our little games. "Please?"

Gray turned the vibrator off and pushed two fingers into me. That worked too. Except he didn't fuck me with his fingers. He drew my juices out and swirled them over the pucker of my ass.

I gasped in a breath, anticipating the push of his fingers there.

"Please what, Angel?"

"Please, fuck me."

"Hmm. I like the sound of that. Fuck you where?"

Now, I'd done it. Here's where the real fun began. "Anywhere you want."

"Say it, love. Tell me where you want me to fuck you. Here," he pushed his fingers back into my pussy. "Or here?"

This time he speared one wet finger through the tight ring of muscles and pumped it slowly into my ass.

My body craved his dark desires. He carefully controlled my every yearning, and we tortured each other a little longer.

"What about the vibrators?"

"Whichever hole you don't choose, that's where your Christmas present is going."

Mierde.

"But if you don't pick soon. I'll decide for you."

I bit my lip considering whether to push him further into this erotic game we were playing or not. It was more fun to drive him crazy. After all, I wanted this to be the best Christmas he'd ever had. "Do it."

"Always trying to top from the bottom, Angel. So, now you get punished. Unlock the cuffs and get on your knees, ass in the air. You're getting a Christmas spanking."

Did I mention I loved Christmas?

FUTURE PERFECT

*L*et me just tell you this. Christmas spankings are the best kind. Trust me.

I got into position and Gray kneeled behind me. His cock pressed into the flesh of my right butt cheek and I loved knowing he was enjoying our game. I was too.

He slid a vibrator through my folds, but it wasn't turned on and he didn't come even close to my clit. One second it was torturing me from below and the next it buzzed against my ass.

"Relax, baby. You can take this, it's not as big as my cock." He didn't wait for me to respond and pushed the head of the vibe into me.

I groaned through the sweet burn of that first penetration. He worked it in and out of me, preparing me, until it was fully inside.

"That is one fucking sexy site. Here. Take the other toy and hold it against your clit. But don't turn it on yet. I get to decide when. You got me?" He pushed the new vibrator into my hand and I immediately placed it right where I needed it most.

"Yes."

"That's earned you an extra spanking. You know what I want to hear."

Yes, I did. But was I going to say it? No, I wasn't. "Yes."

"One more. Say it, Angel." His voice was growing huskier by the moment.

I threw in my final trump card. "Make me."

"Fuck."

Gray pushed his cock into my pussy and thrust into me once, twice, three times before he turned the vibrator in my ass on and smacked my rear. "Say it."

"Yes."

Smack. Thrust, thrust, thrust. "Turn on the vibrator and don't even think about coming until you're ready to say it."

With two vibes going, Gray fucking me, and his hand smacking my ass over and over, my body was on the verge of over stimulation. I needed one last command from his lips. He withheld those words from me like he did my orgasms. The waiting and the need amplified every sensation in my body.

There was only one thing I'd ever needed from him.

To be his.

"Enough." Gray pulled the toy from my ass and his cock from me and for a tiny second I thought I'd goaded him too far.

Before I could think of what to do, his cock pushed into my ass and he took me fast and hard.

"Say. It. Angel. Say you are mine once more."

Holy Virgin Mother of Guadalupe. I cried out my gratification as he drove into me over and over, pushing me higher than we'd ever gone together before. My body wound tighter and tighter, taking the pleasure he was giving to me and returning it to him threefold.

"Gray. I'm yours. Forever. Love you." Those were the words he needed even more than all the Yes, Sirs in the world. We belonged to each other.

"Fuck, yes. Come for me, Angel. I love you so much. Come for me."

Our bodies exploded together, our cries long and loud. The orgasm took me so hard I nearly blacked out and I collapsed all the way to the floor pulling Gray down with me.

He withdrew from my body and wrapped his arms, legs, and shoulders around me under the tree. Our breaths came fast and harsh for an eternity and the pounding of his heart against my back, synced with my own.

I didn't want to close my eyes for fear that I would fall asleep. I wanted this moment to last almost as long as forever.

"Merry Christmas, my Angel."

"*Feliz Navidad*, Gray."

He chuckled and snuggled into me.

We made love again in the shower later while pretending to clean up, and again right before we took a much-needed nap. Both times were vanilla compared to our Christmas romp this morning, and he was soft and sweet.

Afterwards when we laid together in the afterglow of all the day's orgasms, I asked him, "Was that the best Christmas you've had?"

He kissed me on the forehead. "It was by far the best Christmas ever."

"Are you unscrooged?"

"I wouldn't go that far. We could have done this any old day. Didn't need to be Christmas."

I swore a litany at him in Spanish for that.

Good thing I had one more Christmas ghost up my sleeve.

We slept in the next day. Made love again, and around dinner time my last attempt at changing Gray's mind about the holidays was ready to go.

My ghosts of Christmas future had scrambled to get to the island on time, but I'd tempted them with a trip to the local kink club before they jetted back home. No one was complaining.

They loved Gray almost as much as I did.

Around sunset I put the plan into action.

"Gray, let's go for a stroll down the beach before we eat. I feel like we haven't been out of the house for days."

He grabbed my hand automatically and headed for the door. "That's because we haven't been. Not since your Ghost of Christmas Past. I'm glad you're done with your Dickensian plots now."

"Hmm," was all I said to that. I was trying extra hard not to give off any tells that he was in for a visit from one more Christmas.

"Angel. What are you up to?"

Coño. "Nothing."

"Do you need another spanking?"

Luckily, I didn't have to answer that because right then the ghosts of Christmas future showed up as carolers on the beach.

"Good King Wenceslas looked down on the something something. Something something blah blah blah, something baby Jesus."

"Cade. I thought you knew the words to this one." Vanessa curled her arm around her love's and gave him a kiss on the cheek.

He was adorably besotted. "Who is King Wenceslas, anyway?"

"Should we do Frosty the snowman?" Eden asked.

"It seems weird to be singing about a snowy anything on a tropical island." Lilly laughed and snuggled her baby in her arms. "Doesn't it, little guy? Yes, it does."

All of our friends, Cade and Vanessa, Hawk and Lilly and their baby Ilario, Eden and Sawyer, Dominic, Ian, Celine, Addison, Jim, and more, stood in a circle around a twelve-foot pine tree. I'd had it flown in and replanted in a special patch of imported soil on the beach a few days ago. From top to bottom, the tree had sparkling balls and lights.

They hadn't yet noticed us, but Gray looked at every one of them, happy and laughing, having a grand Christmas celebration because they were together. No presents, no snow, not even any mistletoe.

Gray pulled me into his arms. "You did this for me too? This is your ghosts of Christmas future, isn't it?"

"Your Christmases haven't been filled with the love of friends and family. Mine really haven't either. This is what I want for us. I'll never be lonely as long as we're together and I'm content to spend every day, holiday or not with you. Having our friends here makes it that much more special though, don't you think?"

"It does." Gray kissed me, lingering long enough to warm me from the inside out for him.

"Are you still feeling scrooged?"

"No, my love. I'm as happy as an angel. Now let's go say hello to our family."

Phew.

"Then later," he whispered in my ear before we made for the group, "we'll get out your Christmas toys and celebrate all over again."

God, I loved Christmas.

I loved Gray even more.

———

Did you enjoy Gray and Angelina's Christmas fun?
You can read their entire saga starting with
Rebound.
Available on Amazon and in Kindle Unlimited.

NEED MORE GRAY AND ANGEL?

If you haven't already read all of Gray and Angel's adventures, get all the sexy times and feels in the *The Curvy Seduction Saga*.

If you've already enjoyed their story you'll probably like *The Curvy Love Series*. It stars some of the characters you were introduced to in Gray and Angel's world.

Turn the page to keep reading. I've got an excerpt from *Curvy Diversion* for you starring Danica, from the Devils and Angels club.

Want even more curvy girls getting stories of happy ever afters with hot guys?

I've got a present for all my elite readers.

A couple of free ebooks and your very own Curvy Love Adult Coloring book!

Want to sign up for my Curvy Connection newsletter today?

YES?!

Sign up here —> http://geni.us/CurvyConnection

You'll get exclusive excerpts, sneak peeks, contests and

giveaways, get to know me, and receive notifications when my new books come out. Yay!

EXCERPT FROM CURVY DIVERSION

Saturday Night and I Ain't Got Nobody

I wasn't going to Devils and Angels. That felt weird, like there was something I'd forgotten to do.

It's not like I couldn't go without a sub. There was never any shortage of submissive men who wanted me to make them lick my boots or other more fun places. The thought of spending an evening with a beta male held zero appeal at the moment.

A small break from the scene, as recommended, that's all this was. Then I could come back to it with renewed vigor. I even had a challenge in mind. There was a new coffee shop not far from my loft and a very cute latte boy.

But, not tonight. Netflix was queued up with a whole list of chick flicks, the facial-mani-pedi station was set up on my coffee table, the newest trial and error paleo cookie recipe was in the oven and making the house smell delicious, and Nessie was on her way over for girls night in. Everything was perfect and exactly what I needed for some R&R.

The phone rang and Nessie's number popped up. Uh-oh. "Hey Ness."

"Don't hate me." Her tone was apologetic and distracted at the same time.

Not that I could, but I knew already I was in for some alone time. "I'll never hate you. What's come up?" I tried to hide the resignation in my voice.

"I'm sorry. A whole stack of invoices just landed on my desk and not only do they need to be paid yesterday, they are in some weird back-assward order. Ugh, I could just beat my department head for the way he lets people run roughshod over payments."

Kind of like the way she let everyone else in her life walk all over her. If ever anyone needed a vacation, it was Nessie. I had plans for her though. "Bring him on down to the club, I'll be happy to whip him into shape for you."

"Oh, you and that club." She laughed, but only half-heartedly. "Shoot, I'd love to hear your latest escapades, but with this stack of paperwork and the museum board meeting tomorrow at the butt crack of dawn, I'm down for the count."

"Rain check then."

"For sure. If you want we can grab coffee at the new place, what's it called, uh, The Mean Bean, tomorrow after my meeting."

"Yeah. Can't wait. Text me when you're on your way."

I plopped down on the couch and hit play on some romcom about an awkward sexual adventure. The bowl of avocado for our facials cried out for some chips. There would be plenty now.

I was half into spreading the green goo on my face when

the phone beeped a Facetime call at me. Maybe Nessie gave her boss the finger and was on her way.

I slid my thumb across the green button and a face popped up on the screen. But, it wasn't Ness. Unless she'd grown a five o'clock shadow and a penis.

"Dani?"

"Grant?" I dipped the phone so all he could see was my kneecap and scraped as much of the avocado off my face as I could with one big chip, swiping at the rest with my sleeve. "What's the word nerd?"

He was far from a nerd. Looks of a model, but never came out from behind his own camera long enough for anyone to get a picture of him. Although, I had a few shots.

"I was hoping to catch you. Getting ready to go out?" His voice was that low flirty tone I adored.

"Not tonight." I should have lied. He'd know something was up if I wasn't going out on a Saturday night. He and I had torn up the town more than once in our college days.

"Under the weather? You do look a little green." He swiped a finger along his chin a few times.

Crap, I'd missed a huge chunk of facial guac. "Har har. You know the things I do to keep this face looking young and beautiful."

"It's all a mystery to me. But, you do look edible."

That was a little more flirty than Grant usually was with me. Not that he hadn't ever hit on me. But, we'd missed our moment. Either he was attached or I was busy with a sub, not that I'd tell him that. Somewhere along the way we gave up on being lovers and became friends. He was the only other long-term relationship I had with anyone besides Nessie, and the two of them had never even met.

"What're you doing in on a Saturday night? Don't you have some twenty-one year old twig to be seen on the town with? What town are you even in?"

"I'm in Prague, so Saturday night has come and gone, and I haven't... okay maybe I have dated a younger model or two."

"If you call robbing the cradle dating." The man had a thing for younger women. That was fine, I had a thing for younger men. We'd had this convo more than once in the opposite direction.

"It's actually why I called, love."

"To rob my cradle?"

He cleared his throat, nervous-like. "I know this is a long shot, but do you have a job booked for next week?"

The shot wasn't as long as he thought. The jobs were coming fewer and farther between than they used to. I certainly wasn't ready to retire at thirty-three, but I wasn't being booked like I used to. "You're in luck, I'm free. You got something for me?"

"Kind of. I'm calling in a favor Dans. Can you fly out to Costa Rica Monday morning? Stay at least three days?"

"Are you kidding me? Costa Rica? Please. I'd take that job for free. You're shooting? Who's it for?" I'd worked with Grant a few times over the years, but he did mostly the kind of high-fashion that didn't include plus-size.

"Actually. It would be for free. I can't pay you and I can't guarantee the photos will even make it into Sports magazine."

Umm. Grant and his family were kazillionaires. Maybe this was for charity. "A. Sports magazine doesn't do plus size models in swimsuits or otherwise, and B. Why can't you pay?"

"Here's the favor part. I'm doing a proposal to dear old dad that this year we do an all bodies swimsuit edition, but I've got to foot the bill myself. I'll cover flights and hotel, but, I'm beg, borrowing, and stealing models."

That I could get down with. Too few magazines believed that all bodies were beautiful and my heart pitter pattered at the fact that Grant wanted to do something about it.

"Your dad will never go for it. I love him, Grant, but he isn't exactly known for proponenting realistic standards of beauty. I mean, look at step-monster, what, number three was it? She was more silicone than the valley."

"I know, I know. But, I'm taking over G-Media at the new year and if I could get him to agree to this new look now, it will be a thousand percent easier to get the board behind me in January when I make more changes to the magazines. And it was number four."

Holy news flash. "Wait, what? You're taking over Granted Media? When did this happen?"

"My father asked me to become the new CEO starting in January." His tone was that of a kid who had to come in for dinner right in the middle of an exciting game of kiss the girls.

"The billionaire playboy settles down and takes an office, huh?" Grant's father had been trying to control him, and failing since we were in school together. What I didn't understand was why he was giving in now.

"I have to. It's all hush hush for the moment, but dad had a series of what they're calling mini-strokes this year and he decided to step down." Grant's face through the phone was sad and resigned.

That boy had a myriad of conflicting emotions about this situation that I could see written all over him like a giant neon sign saying – ask me about my guilt.

None of his girlfriends would see that. Only the ca-ching of cashing in on their billionaire CEO boyfriends moneybags who could advance their careers.

Grant had called me out on questionable career choices. That's what friends were for.

"Do you want the job?" I asked.

It would be a serious cramp in his wham-bam-thankyou-ma'am lifestyle. But it also meant he'd be moving to town. Granted Media's HQ was within walking distance from my loft.

He was my second best friend in the whole world, but partly because we only saw each other a few times a year. He was separate from my everyday life, and I liked it that way. A girl had to keep some mystery about her, even from her friends.

"Yes. Maybe. Kind of." He swiped a hand over his face and then grinned sideways at me through the phone. "Can we save that conversation for later? For example, on a beach in Costa Rica with a fruity drink in hand?"

I was totally down for the gig, paid or not. What better way to take a vacation than at a tropical resort, where there were no BDSM clubs or subs or Doms in sight or Dommes for that matter. Fun times with Grant were an added bonus. Maybe I could work out my feelings about him moving to my neck of the woods while we were at it.

"I'm not letting you off the hook, but yes. What's up with the change to using diverse models? That's so not Granted." I never ever thought I'd work for any of their magazines. They weren't really my people. By which I meant humans with an actual body fat percentage.

"But, it needs to be. We're behind the times and the circulation is showing it. Only about half the magazines have a strong online presence and the look of every one of the print rags is outdated. I don't want to see the business my grandfather built dissolve because a bunch of old fuddy-duddies still think Twiggy is in."

"Did you just say fuddy-duddies?" He was either acting nine years old or seventy-nine. That or he was already turning into one of those corporate politically correct types. God, I hoped not. I liked the don't-do-anything-I-wouldn't-do-and-I've-done-a-shit-ton guy I'd had a crush on in college way more

"Better than dirty bastards. They're slow to change their underpants, much less the magazine. I want to start with Sports and transition all the magazines into something current."

"You're saying *L'eau* isn't going to feature the heroin chic models that make a size zero look baggy anymore?" Not bitter at all. Nooooo.

"I'm saying that I've got a chance to bring the antiquated ideals in both body and business the board of Granted Media has been operating on since the 70s into the modern world. I'm not saying it will happen overnight."

Ooh. He already sounded like the sexy CEO from all my naughty romance novels.

"Even your porno mags?" That would be the day.

"Ahem, they are men's magazines, and they have great articles, I'll have you know." He waggled his eyebrows at me.

"Oh, yes, because everyone reads them for the articles."

"Not to mention the tits and ass."

"You're an ass."

"You've got great tits." His eyes dropped to the front of my shirt.

I couldn't decide whether to preen or tell him to fuck off. I went with ignore it. "I'll be there for you, you know I will. When and where?"

"Check your email. I sent a link to your e-ticket to San Jose and hotel reservation in Montezuma. We'll be shooting on Tortuga Island."

I popped up the email app and scrolled through the junk mail to Grant's message. "This says the ticket was purchased yesterday."

"I told you I knew you'd say yes."

Of course I would. It was Grant. "And what if I hadn't?"

"Blackmail of old pictures of you with green goo on your face and curlers in your hair from fifteen years ago posted on every social media site in the world."

"You do not have those in digital."

"I do now."

A message popped up on my screen with a picture icon. I clicked to enlarge and… "Eek."

He had a screenshot of ten minutes ago next to a scan of a picture from our sophomore year. Same green goo.

"See you Monday, love?"

"I'll be there with bells and whistles on."

"Hopefully less than that." Grant winked.

He meant the swimsuits from the designers, right? No way he was asking me to take my clothes off for him. Nuh-uh. Of course not. He was in a mood from the pressure of having to take over and pretending everything was sweetness and light. That's why I was getting this weird vibe from him.

We clicked off and I began mentally packing. I wouldn't

need much for the island. A swimsuit, a sundress, some capris, lots and lots and lots of sunscreen. I had plenty of freckles as it was, and I was not going to come home with a burn.

This was exactly what I needed. Talk about perfect timing. A few days in the sun and surf would get my mind off power relationships.

I didn't need them when it came to Grant.

Continue the story, grab *Curvy Diversion* on Amazon or in Kindle Unlimited.

ALSO BY AIDY AWARD

The Curvy Love Series

Curvy Diversion

Curvy Temptation

Curvy Persuasion

The Curvy Seduction Saga

Rebound

Rebellion

Reignite

Rejoice

Revel

Dragons Love Curves

Chase Me

Tease Me

Unmask Me

Bite Me

Cage Me

Baby Me

Defy Me

Surprise Me

Dirty Dragon

Crave Me

Slay Me

Alpha Wolves Want Curves

Dirty Wolf

Naughty Wolf

Kinky Wolf

Merry Wolf

ABOUT THE AUTHOR

Aidy Award is a curvy girl who kind of has a thing for stormtroopers. She's also the author of the popular Curvy Love series and the hot new Dragons Love Curves series. She writes curvy girl erotic romance, about real love, and dirty fun, with happy ever afters because every woman deserves great sex and even better romance, no matter her size, shape, or what the scale says.

Read the delicious tales of hot heroes and curvy heroines come to life under the covers and between the pages of Aidy's books. Then let her know because she really does want to hear from her readers.

Connect with Aidy on her website. www.AidyAward.com get her Curvy Connection, and join her Facebook Group - Aidy's Amazeballs.

Made in the USA
Middletown, DE
04 May 2022